NICOLA BARKER

Heading Inland

FOURTH ESTATE • London

Fourth Estate
An imprint of HarperCollins*Publishers*
77–85 Fulham Palace Road
Hammersmith
London w6 8jb

This Fourth Estate paperback edition published 2011
1

First published in Great Britain by Faber and Faber Ltd in 1996

'Bendy-Linda' first appeared in *Critical Quarterly*

Nicola Barker asserts the moral right to be identified as the author of this work

A catalogue record for this book is available from the British Library

ISBN 978-0-00-743571-5

Typeset by Palimpsest Book Production Limited,
Falkirk, Stirlingshire

Printed and bound in Great Britain by Clays Ltd, St Ives plc

MIX
Paper from
responsible sources
FSC C007454

FSC
www.fsc.org

FSC™ is a non-profit international organisation established to promote
the responsible management of the world's forests. Products carrying the
FSC label are independently certified to assure consumers that they come
from forests that are managed to meet the social, economic and
ecological needs of present and future generations,
and other controlled sources.

Find out more about HarperCollins and the environment at
www.harpercollins.co.uk/green

Contents

With thanks to
the Arts Council of Great Britain
for the Writer's Award (1994/5)
without which this book would not
have been completed.

For my mother

Inside Information

Martha's social worker was under the impression that by getting herself pregnant, Martha was looking for an out from a life of crime.

She couldn't have been more wrong.

'First thing I ever nicked,' Martha bragged, when her social worker was initially assigned to her, 'very first thing I ever stole was a packet of Lil-lets. I told the store detective I took them as a kind of protest. You pay 17½ per cent VAT on every single box. Men don't pay it on razors, you know, which is absolutely bloody typical.'

'But you stole other things, too, on that occasion, Martha.'

'Fags and a bottle of Scotch. So what?' she grinned. 'Pay VAT on those too, don't you?'

Martha's embryo was unhappy about its assignment to Martha. Early on, just after conception, it appealed to the higher body responsible for its selection and placement. This caused something of a scandal in the After-Life. The World-Soul was consulted – a democratic body of pin-pricks of light, an enormous institution – which came, unusually enough, to a rapid decision.

'Tell the embryo,' they said, 'hard cheese.'

The embryo's social worker relayed this information

through a system of vibrations – a language which embryos alone in the Living World can produce and receive. Martha felt these conversations only as tiny spasms and contractions.

Being pregnant was good, Martha decided, because store detectives were much more sympathetic when she got caught. Increasingly, they let her off with a caution after she blamed her bad behaviour on dodgy hormones.

The embryo's social worker reasoned with the embryo that all memories of the After-Life and feelings of uncertainty about placement were customarily eradicated during the trauma of birth. This was a useful expedient. 'Naturally,' he added, 'the nine-month wait is always difficult, especially if you've drawn the short straw in allocation terms, but at least by the time you've battled your way through the cervix, you won't remember a thing.'

The embryo replied, snappily, that it had never believed in the maxim that Ignorance is Bliss. But the social worker (a corgi in its previous incarnation) re-stated that the World Soul's decision was final.

As a consequence, the embryo decided to take things into its own hands. It would communicate with Martha while it still had the chance and offer her, if not an incentive, at the very least a moral imperative.

Martha grew larger during a short stint in Wormwood Scrubs. She was seven months gone on her day of release. The embryo was now a well-formed foetus, and, if its penis was any indication, it was a boy. He calculated that he had, all things being well, eight weeks to change the course of Martha's life.

You see, the foetus was special. He had an advantage

over other, similarly situated, disadvantaged foetuses. This foetus had Inside Information.

In the After-Life, after his sixth or seventh incarnation, the foetus had worked for a short spate as a troubleshooter for a large pharmaceutical company. During the course of his work and research, he had stumbled across something so enormous, something so terrible about the World-Soul, that he'd been compelled to keep this information to himself, for fear of retribution.

The rapidity of his assignment as Martha's future baby was, in part, he was convinced, an indication that the World-Soul was aware of his discoveries. His soul had been snatched and implanted in Martha's belly before he'd even had a chance to discuss the matter rationally. In the womb, however, the foetus had plenty of time to analyse his predicament. *It was a cover-up!* He was being gagged, brainwashed and railroaded into another life sentence on earth.

In prison, Martha had been put on a sensible diet and was unable to partake of the fags and the sherry and the Jaffa cakes which were her normal dietary staples. The foetus took this opportunity to consume as many vital calories and nutrients as possible. He grew at a considerable rate, exercised his knees, his feet, his elbows, ballooned out Martha's belly with nudges and pokes.

In his seventh month, on their return home, the foetus put his plan into action. He angled himself in Martha's womb, at just the right angle, and with his foot, gave the area behind Martha's belly button a hefty kick. On the outside, Martha's belly was already a considerable size. Her stomach was about as round as it could be, and her navel, which usually stuck inwards, had popped outwards, like a nipple.

By kicking the inside of her navel at just the correct angle, the foetus – using his Inside Information – had successfully popped open the lid of Martha's belly button like it was an old-fashioned pill-box.

Martha noticed that her belly button was ajar while she was taking a shower. She opened its lid and peered inside. She couldn't have been more surprised. Under her belly button was a small, neat zipper, constructed out of delicate bones. She turned off the shower, grabbed hold of the zipper and pulled it. It unzipped vertically, from the middle of her belly to the top. Inside, she saw her foetus, floating in brine. 'Hello,' the foetus said. 'Could I have a quick word with you, please?'

'This is incredible!' Martha exclaimed, closing the zipper and opening it again. The foetus put out a restraining hand. 'If you'd just hang on a minute I could tell you how this was possible . . .'

'It's so weird!' Martha said, closing the zipper and getting dressed.

Martha went to Tesco's. She picked up the first three items that came to hand, unzipped her stomach and popped them inside. On her way out, she set off the alarms – the bar-codes activated them, even from deep inside her – but when she was searched and scrutinized and interrogated, no evidence could be found of her hidden booty. Martha told the security staff that she'd consider legal action if they continued to harass her in this way.

When she got home, Martha unpacked her womb. The foetus, squashed into a corner, squeezed up against a tin of Spam and a packet of sponge fingers, was intensely irritated by what he took to be Martha's unreasonable behaviour.

'You're not the only one who has a zip, you know,' he said. 'All pregnant women have them; it's only a question of finding out how to use them, from the outside, gaining the knowledge. But the World-Soul has kept this information hidden since the days of Genesis, when it took Adam's rib and reworked it into a zip with a pen-knife.'

'Shut it,' Martha said. 'I don't want to hear another peep from you until you're born.'

'But I'm trusting you,' the foetus yelled, 'with this information. It's my salvation!'

She zipped up.

Martha went shopping again. She shopped sloppily at first, indiscriminately, in newsagents, clothes shops, hardware stores, chemists. She picked up what she could and concealed it in her belly.

The foetus grew disillusioned. He re-opened negotiations with his social worker. 'Look,' he said, 'I know something about the World-Soul which I'm willing to divulge to my earth-parent Martha if you don't abort me straight away.'

'You're too big now,' the social worker said, fingering his letter of acceptance to the Rotary Club which preambled World-Soul membership. 'And anyway, it strikes me that Martha isn't much interested in what you have to say.'

'Do you honestly believe,' the foetus asked, 'that any woman on earth in her right mind would consider a natural birth if she knew that she could simply unzip?'

The social worker replied coldly: 'Women are not kangaroos, you cheeky little foetus. If the World Soul has chosen to keep the zipper quiet then it will have had the best of reasons for doing so.'

'But if babies were unzipped and taken out when they're ready,' the foetus continued, 'then there would be no trauma, no memory loss. Fear of death would be a thing of the past. We could eradicate the misconception of a Vengeful God.'

'And all the world would go to hell,' the social worker said.

'How can you say that?'

The foetus waited for a reply, but none came.

Martha eventually sorted out her priorities. She shopped in Harrods and Selfridges and Liberty's. She became adept at slotting things of all conceivable shapes and sizes into her belly. Unfortunately, the foetus himself was growing quite large. After being unable to fit in a spice rack, Martha unzipped and addressed him directly. 'Is there any possibility,' she asked, 'that I might be able to take you out prematurely so that there'd be more room in there?'

The foetus stared back smugly. 'I'll come out,' he said firmly, 'when I'm good and ready.'

Before she could zip up, he added, 'And when I do come out, I'm going to give you the longest and most painful labour in Real-Life history. I'm going to come out sideways, doing the can-can.'

Martha's hand paused, momentarily, above the zipper. 'Promise to come out very quickly,' she said, 'and I'll nick you some baby clothes.'

The foetus snorted in a derisory fashion. 'Revolutionaries,' he said, 'don't wear baby clothes. Steal me a gun, though, and I'll fire it through your spleen.'

Martha zipped up quickly, shocked at this vindictive

6

little bundle of vituperation she was unfortunate enough to be carrying. She smoked an entire packet of Marlboro in one sitting, and smirked, when she unzipped, just slightly, at the coughing which emerged.

The foetus decided that he had no option but to rely on his own natural wit and guile to foil both his mother and the forces of the After-Life. He began to secrete various items that Martha stole in private little nooks and crannies about her anatomy.

On the last night of his thirty-sixth week, he put his plan into action. In his arsenal: an indelible pen, a potato, a large piece of cotton from the hem of a dress, a thin piece of wire from the supports of a bra, all craftily reassembled. In the dead of night, while Martha was snoring, he gradually worked the zip open from the inside, and did what he had to do.

The following morning, blissfully unaware of the previous night's activities, Martha went out shopping to Marks and Spencer's. She picked up some Belgian chocolates and a bottle of port, took hold of her zipper and tried to open her belly. It wouldn't open. The zipper seemed smaller and more difficult to hold.

'That bastard,' she muttered, 'must be jamming it up from the inside.' She put down her booty and headed for the exit. On her way out of the shop, she set off the alarms.

'For Chrissakes!' she told the detective, 'I've got nothing on me!' And for once, she meant it.

Back home, Martha attacked her belly with a pair of nail scissors. But the zip wasn't merely jammed, it was meshing and merging and disappearing, fading like the tail end of a bruise. She was frazzled. She looked around for her cigarettes. She found her packet and opened it. The last couple had gone, and instead, inside, was a note.

Martha, [the note said] *I have made good my escape, fully intact. I sewed a pillow into your belly. On the wall of your womb I've etched and inked an indelible bar-code. Thanks for the fags.*
Love, Baby.

'But you can't do that!' Martha yelled. 'You don't have the technology!' She thought she heard a chuckle, behind her. She span around. On the floor, under the table, she saw a small lump of afterbirth, tied up into a neat parcel by an umbilical cord. She could smell a whiff of cigarette smoke. She thought she heard laughter, outside the door, down the hall. She listened intently, but heard nothing more.

G-String

Ever fallen out with somebody simply because they agreed with you? Well, this is exactly what happened to Gillian and her pudgy but reliable long-term date, Mr Kip.

They lived separately in Canvey Island. Mr Kip ran a small but flourishing insurance business there. Gillian worked for a car-hire firm in Grays Thurrock. She commuted daily.

Mr Kip – he liked to be called that, an affectation, if you will – was an ardent admirer of the great actress Katharine Hepburn. She was skinny and she was elegant and she was sparky and she was intelligent. Everything a girl should be. She was *old* now, too, Gillian couldn't help thinking, but naturally she didn't want to appear a spoilsport so she kept her lips sealed.

Gillian was thirty-four, a nervous size sixteen, had no cheekbones to speak of and hair which she tried to perm. God knows she tried. She was the goddess of frizz. She frizzed but she did not fizz. She was not fizzy like Katharine. At least, that's what Mr Kip told her.

Bloody typical, isn't it? When a man chooses to date a woman, long term, who resembles his purported heroine in no way whatsoever? Is it safe? Is it cruel? Is it downright simple-minded?

Gillian did her weekly shopping in Southend. They had

everything you needed there. Of course there was the odd exception: fishing tackle, seaside mementos, insurance, underwear. These items she never failed to purchase in Canvey Island itself, just to support local industry.

A big night out was on the cards. Mr Kip kept telling her how big it would be. A local Rotary Club do, and Gillian was to be Mr Kip's special partner, he was to escort her, in style. He was even taking the cloth off his beloved old Aston Martin for the night to drive them there and back. And he'd never deigned to do that before. Previously he'd only ever taken her places in his H-reg Citroën BX.

Mr Kip told Gillian that she was to buy a new frock for this special occasion. Something, he imagined, like that glorious dress Katharine Hepburn wore during the bar scene in her triumph, *Bringing Up Baby*.

Dutifully, Gillian bought an expensive dress in white chiffon which didn't at all suit her. Jeanie – twenty-one with doe eyes, sunbed-brown and weighing in at ninety pounds – told Gillian that the dress made her look like an egg-box. All lumpyhumpy. It was her underwear, Jeanie informed her – If only! Gillian thought – apparently it was much too visible under the dress's thin fabric. Jeanie and Gillian were conferring in The Lace Bouquet, the lingerie shop on Canvey High Street where Jeanie worked.

'I tell you what,' Jeanie offered, 'all in one lace bodysuit, right? Stretchy stuff. No bra. No knickers. It'll hold you in an' everything.' Jeanie held up the prospective item. Bodysuits, Gillian just *knew*, would not be Mr Kip's idea of sophisticated. She shook her head. She looked down at her breasts. 'I think I'll need proper support,' she said, grimacing.

Jeanie screwed up her eyes and chewed at the tip of her thumb. 'Bra and pants, huh?'

'I think so.'

Although keen not to incur Jeanie's wrath, Gillian picked out the kind of bra she always wore, in bright, new white, and a pair of matching briefs.

Jeanie ignored the bra. It was functional. Fair enough. But the briefs she held aloft and proclaimed, 'Passion killers.'

'They're tangas,' Gillian said, defensively, proud of knowing the modern technical term for the cut-away pant. 'They're brief briefs.'

Jeanie snorted. 'No one wears these things any more, Gillian. There's enough material here to launch a sailboat.'

Jeanie picked up something that resembled an obscenely elongated garter and proffered it to Gillian. Gillian took hold of the scrap.

'What's this?'

'G-string.'

'My God, girls wear these in Dave Lee Roth videos.'

'Who's that?' Jeanie asked, sucking in her cheeks, insouciant.

'They aren't practical,' Gillian said.

Jeanie's eyes narrowed. 'These are truly modern knickers,' she said. 'These are what *everyone* wears now. And I'll tell you for why. No visible pantie line!'

Gillian didn't dare inform her that material was the whole point of a pantie. Wasn't it?

Oh hell, Gillian thought, shifting on Mr Kip's Aston Martin's leather seats, maybe I should've worn it in for a few days first. It felt like her G-string was making headway from between her buttocks up into her throat. She felt like a leg of lamb, trussed up with cheese wire.

Now she knew how a horse felt when offered a new bit and bridle for the first time.

'Wearing hairspray?' Mr Kip asked, out of the blue.

'What?'

'If you are,' he said, ever careful, 'then don't lean your head back on to the seat. It's real leather and you may leave a stain.'

Gillian bit her lip and stopped wriggling.

'Hope it doesn't rain,' Mr Kip added, keeping his hand on the gearstick in a very male way, 'the wipers aren't quite one hundred per cent.'

Oh, the G-string was a modern thing, but it looked so horrid! Gillian wanted to be a modern girl but when she espied her rear-end engulfing the slither of string like a piece of dental floss entering the gap between two great white molars, her heart sank down into her strappy sandals. It tormented her. Like the pain of an old bunion, it quite took off her social edge.

When Mr Kip didn't remark favourably on her new dress; when, in fact, he drew a comparison between Gillian and the cone-shaped upstanding white napkins on the fancily made-up Rotary tables, she almost didn't try to smile. He drank claret. He smoked a cigar and tipped ash on her. He didn't introduce her to any of his Rotary friends. Normally, Gillian might have grimaced on through. But tonight she was a modern girl in torment and this kind of behaviour quite simply would not do.

Of course she didn't actually *say* anything. Mr Kip finally noticed Gillian's distress during liqueurs.

'What's got into you?'

'Headache,' Gillian grumbled, fighting to keep her hands on her lap.

Two hours later, Mr Kip deigned to drive them home.

It was raining. Gillian fastened her seatbelt. Mr Kip switched on the windscreen wipers. They drove in silence. Then all of a sudden, *wheeeuwoing*! One of the wipers flew off the windscreen and into a ditch. Mr Kip stopped the car. He reversed. He clambered out to look for the wiper, but because he wore glasses, drops of rain impaired his vision.

It was a quiet road. What the hell. Mr Kip told Gillian to get out and look for it.

'In my white dress?' Gillian asked, quite taken aback.

Fifteen minutes later, damp, mussed, muddy, Gillian finally located the wiper. Mr Kip fixed it back on, but when he turned the relevant switch on the dash, neither of the wipers moved. He cursed like crazy.

'Well, that's that,' he said, and glared at Gillian like it was her fault completely. They sat and sat. It kept right on raining.

Finally Gillian couldn't stand it a minute longer. 'Give me your tie,' she ordered. Mr Kip grumbled but did as she'd asked. Gillian clambered out of the car and attached the tie to one of the wipers.

'OK,' she said, trailing the rest of the tie in through Mr Kip's window. 'Now we need something else. Are you wearing a belt?'

Mr Kip shook his head.

'Something long and thin,' Gillian said, 'like a rope.'

Mr Kip couldn't think of anything.

'Shut your eyes,' Gillian said. Mr Kip shut his eyes, but after a moment, naturally, he peeped.

And what a sight! Gillian laboriously freeing herself from some panties which looked as bare and sparse and confoundedly stringy as a pirate's eye patch.

'Good gracious!' Mr Kip exclaimed. 'You could at least

have worn some French knickers or cami-knickers or something proper. Those are preposterous!'

Gillian turned on him. 'I've really had it with you, Colin,' she snarled, 'with your silly, affected, old-fashioned car and clothes and *everything*.'

From her bag Gillian drew out her Swiss Army Knife and applied it with gusto to the plentiful elastic on her G-string. Then she tied one end to the second wiper and pulled the rest around and through her window. 'Right,' she said, 'start up the engine.'

Colin Kip did as he was told. Gillian manipulated the wipers manually; left, right, left, right. All superior and rhythmical and practical and dour-faced.

Mr Kip was very impressed. He couldn't help himself. After several minutes of driving in silence he took his hand off the gearstick and slid it on to Gillian's lap.

'Watch it,' Gillian said harshly. 'Don't you dare provoke me, Colin. I haven't put my Swiss Army Knife away yet.'

She felt the pressure of his hand leave her thigh. She was knickerless. She was victorious. She was a truly modern female.

The Three Button Trick

Jack had won Carrie's heart with that old three button trick.

At the genesis of every winter, Jack would bring out his sturdy but ancient grey duffel coat and massage the toggles gently with the tips of his fingers. He'd pick off any fluff or threads from its rough fabric, brush it down vigorously with the flat of his hand and then gradually ease his way into it. One arm, two arms, shift it on to his shoulders, balance it right – the tips of the sleeves both perfectly level with each wrist – then straighten the collar.

Finally, the toggles. The most important part. He'd do them one-handed, pretending, even to himself, some kind of casualness, a studied – if fallacious – preoccupation, his eyes unfocused, imagining, for example, how it felt when he was a small boy learning to tell the time. His father had shown him: ten past, quarter past, see the little hand? See the big hand? But he hadn't learned. It simply didn't click.

So Jack's mother took over instead. She had her own special approach. The way she saw it, any child would learn anything if they thought there was something in it for them: a kiss or a toy or a cookie.

Jack's mother baked Jack a Clock Cake. Each five-minute interval on the cake's perimeter was marked with a tangy, candied, lemon segment. The first slice was taken from the midday or midnight point at the very top of the cake and extended to the first lemon segment on the right, which, Jack learned, signified five minutes past the hour. 'If the little hand is on the twelve,' his mother told him, 'then your slice takes the big hand to five minutes past twelve.'

Jack wrinkled up his nose. 'How about if I have a ten past twelve slice?' he suggested.

He got what he'd asked for.

Jack was born in Wisconsin but moved to London in his early twenties and got a job as a theatrical producer. He'd already worked extensively off-off Broadway. He met Carrie waiting for a bus on a Sunday afternoon outside the National Portrait Gallery. It was the winter of 1972. He was wearing his duffel coat.

Carrie was a blonde who wore her hair in big curls, had milk-pudding skin and breasts like a roomy verandah on the front of her body's smart Georgian townhouse frame. Close up she smelled like a bowl of Multi-flavoured Cheerios.

Before Jack had even smelled her, though, he smiled at her. She smiled in return, glanced away – as girls are wont to do – and then glanced back again. Just as he'd hoped, her eyes finally settled on the toggles on his coat. She pointed. She grinned. 'Your buttons . . .'

'Huh?'

'The buttons on your coat. You've done them up all wrong.'

He looked down and pretended surprise. 'I have?'

Jack held his hands aloft, limply, gave her a watery smile but made no attempt to righten them. Carrie, in turn, put her hand to her curls. She imagined that Jack must be enormously clever to be so vague. Maybe a scientist or a schoolteacher at a boys' private school or maybe a philosophy graduate. Not for a moment did it dawn on her that he might be a fool. And that was sensible, because he was no fool.

Carrie met Sydney two decades later, while attending self-defence classes. Sydney had long, auburn ringlets and freckles and glasses. She was Australian. Her father owned a vineyard just outside Brisbane. Sydney was a sub-editor on a bridal magazine. She was strong and bare and shock-ingly independent. On the back of her elbows, Carrie noticed, the skin was especially thick and in the winter she had to apply Vaseline to this area because otherwise her skin chapped and cracked and became inflamed. The reason, Sydney informed Carrie, that her elbows got so chapped, was that she was very prone to resting her weight on them when she sat at her desk, and also, late at night, when she lay in bed reading or thinking, sometimes for hours.

Sydney was thirty years old and an insomniac. Had been since puberty. As a teenager she'd kept busy during the long night hours memorizing the type-of-grape in the type-of-wine, from-which-vineyard and of-what-vintage. Also she collected wine labels which she stuck into a special jotter.

Nowadays, however, she'd spend her wakeful night-times thinking about broader subjects: men she met, men she fancied, men she'd dated, men she'd two-timed, and if none of these subjects seemed pertinent or topical – during the dry season, as she called it – well, then she'd think about her friends and their lives and how her life connected with theirs and what they both wanted and what they were doing wrong and how and why.

Carrie appreciated Sydney's attentiveness. If Jack had been working late, if Jack kept mentioning the name of an actress, if Jack told her that her skin looked sallow or her roots were showing, well, then she would tell Sydney about it and Sydney would spend the early hours of every morning, resting on her elbows and mulling it all over.

Sydney had a suspicion that Jack was up to something anti-matrimonial and had hinted as much to Carrie. Hinted, but nothing more. Carrie, however, took only what she wanted from Sydney's observations and left the rest. In conversational terms, she was a fussy eater.

Jack walked out on Carrie after twenty-one years of marriage, two days before her forty-fourth birthday. The following night, after he'd packed up and gone, she and Sydney skipped their karate class and sat in the leisure centre's bar instead. Sydney ordered two bottles of Bordeaux. She wasn't in the least bit perturbed by Carrie's predicament. In fact, she was almost pleased because she'd anticipated that this would happen a while ago and was secretly gratified by the wholesale accuracy of her prediction.

'You're still a babe, Carrie,' Sydney whispered, pouring her some more wine. 'You could have any man.'

'I don't want any man,' Carrie whimpered. 'I only want Jack. Only Jack. Only him.'

'That guy Alan,' Sydney noted, 'who takes the Judo class. I know he likes you. Sometimes it seems like his eyes are stuck to your tits with adhesive.'

'Please!'

'It's true.'

'Jack only walked out yesterday, Sydney, probably for a girl fifteen years my junior. You really think I care about anything else at the moment?'

Sydney had great legs; long and lithe and small-kneed. Gazelle legs, llama legs. She crossed them.

'I'm simply observing that Jack isn't the only shark in the ocean.'

Carrie took a tissue from her sports bag and dusted her cheeks with it.

'I remember the very first time I ever met Jack, waiting for a bus outside the National Portrait Gallery. A Sunday afternoon. He had his coat buttoned up all wrong and I pointed it out to him and we started talking . . .' Carrie stopped speaking and hiccuped.

Sydney chewed her bottom lip. That old three button trick, she was thinking. The slimy bastard.

'You know, Carrie,' she said sweetly. 'You're still so beautiful. You're still the biggest lily in the pond. You're still floating on the surface and bright enough to catch the attention of any insect or amphibian that might just happen to be passing.' She paused. 'Even a heron,' she added, as an afterthought.

Carrie scrabbled in her sports bag. She grabbed her purse, opened it, took out a twenty-pound note to pay the barman for the bottles of wine.

'My treat,' Sydney interjected.

Carrie paid him anyway. She was about to shut her purse but then paused and delved inside it.

'Look,' she said, her voice trembling, holding aloft a blue card.

Sydney put out her hand. 'What is it?'

'Our season ticket to the ballet. We went every week. It was one of those routines . . .'

'Well,' Sydney took the ticket and perused it, 'you shall go to the ball, Cinders.'

'What?'

'You and me. We'll go together. When is it?'

'Wednesday.'

Sydney handed the card back. 'Fine.'

As it turned out, Sydney couldn't make it. She rang Carrie at the last minute. Carrie answered the phone wrapped up in a towel, pink from a hot bath.

'What? You can't make it?'

'But I want you to go, anyway. Find someone else.'

'There is no one else. It doesn't matter, though. I wasn't really in the mood myself.'

'Carrie, you've got to go. Alone if needs be. It's the principle of the thing.'

'I know, but it's just . . .'

'What?'

'It's kind of like a regular box and we share it with some other people and if I go alone . . .'

'So? That's great. It means you won't feel entirely isolated, which is ideal.'

'And then there's this fat old man called Heinz who's always there. A complete bore. We really hate him.'

'Heinz?'

'Yes. Jack always found him such a pain. We even tried to get a transfer . . .'

'Bollocks. Just go. Ignore him. What's the ballet?'

'*Petrushka.*'

'Yip!'

'I've seen it before. It's not one of my particular favourites.'

'Go anyway. You've got to start forging your own path, Carrie. You'll thank me after. Honestly.'

She'd made a special effort, with her hair and her make-up. She was wearing a dress that she'd bought for the previous Christmas. It was a glittery burgundy colour. Her lips matched. The box was empty when she arrived. She felt stupid. She sat down.

After five minutes, a couple she knew only to say hello to arrived and took their seats. They smiled and nodded at Carrie. She did the same in return. She then paged through her programme and pretended that she wasn't overhearing their conversation about the kind of conseratory they should build on to the back of their house. He wanted a big one that could fit a table to seat at least six. She wanted a small, bright retreat full of orchids and tomato plants.

Carrie kept reading and re-reading the names of the principal dancers. The orchestra's preparatory honking and parping jangled in her throat and with her nerves. She closed her eyes. I will count to ten. One, two, three, four . . .

'Ooof! Here we go, here we go!'

Heinz, squeezing his way over to his seat, pushing his considerable bulk between the two rows of chairs.

'Oi! Hup! There we are.'

Carrie opened her eyes and stared at him. He had a box of chocolate brazils in one hand and a bulging Selfridges bag in the other, which he almost, but couldn't quite, fit into the gap between his knees and the front of the box.

Carrie's gut rumbled her antipathy. He smelled, always – as Jack had noted on many an occasion – of wine gums and Deep Heat. An old smell. He must have been in his eighties, wore a grey-brown toupee and weighed in, she guessed, like a prize bull, at around three hundred and twenty pounds.

Carrie converted this weight into stone and then back again to occupy herself.

Heinz nodded at her. She nodded back. He always wore a sludge-coloured bow tie. It hung like a shiny little brown turd, poised under his chin.

Heinz endeavoured, with a great harrumphing, to find adequate room by his knees for his bag. 'Uh-oh! Uh-oh!'

Carrie gritted her teeth.

'If you haven't room for your shopping, this chair is empty.' She indicated Jack's empty seat which separated them.

'Empty? Really? That lovely man of yours isn't with you tonight? Empty, you say?' He wheezed as he spoke, like an asthmatic Persian feline, which made his German accent even more pronounced.

You'd think, Carrie speculated, that a wheeze would take the hard edges off a German accent, but you'd be wrong to think so.

'Would you mind' – close to her ear – 'if I sat next to you and put my bag on the other seat?'

My God! Carrie thought, fixing her eyes on the stage curtains and breathing a sigh of relief at their preliminary twitchings.

'Brazil?'

Ten minutes in, Heinz was whispering to her.

'What?'

'Brazil? Go on. Have one.'

'No, thank you.'

'Go on!'

'No. I don't actually like brazils. Nuts give me hives.'

Heinz closed the box and rested it on his lap.

During the intermission, Heinz regaled Carrie with tales about the relative exclusivity of the Turner and Booker prizes. He liked the opera, it turned out, especially

Mozart. He found camomile tea to be excellent for sleep-lessness. He was a widower of seven years.

Carrie noticed how the box's other regulars smiled at her sympathetically whenever they caught her eye. It was odd, really, because actually, with increased acquaintance, Heinz wasn't all that bad. In fact, if anything, he'd made her the centre of attention in the box. The focus, the axis. She felt rather like Princess Margaret opening a day care centre in Fulham.

As the safety curtain rose for the second half, Heinz was telling Carrie how he'd just been to Selfridges to buy a cappuccino maker. He loved everything Italian. He'd been stationed there during the war.

As the stage curtains closed, Heinz mopped something from the corner of his eye and muttered gutturally, 'Poor, poor old Petrushka!'

During the curtain calls Heinz told Carrie that he often felt that it was sadder to be a sad puppet than a sad person.

'Pardon?'

'Petrushka, the puppet. Sometimes it feels like the ballet is sadder because he is a puppet and not a living being.'

'Oh, right. Yes.' Carrie finished applauding and leaned over to pick up her bag. Heinz stayed where he was.

'How will you be getting home then, Carrie?'

'I brought my car.'

'Really?'

'Yes.'

'So maybe, maybe you wouldn't mind joining an old man for a cup of coffee somewhere before you make your way back?'

'Uh?' Carrie was agog.

'Oh! Um . . .' She thought about it for a long moment.

She imagined her quiet house, her empty bed. 'OK,' she said cheerfully, 'love to.'

Sydney was late for Thursday's class so they didn't have a chance to chat beforehand. Afterwards though, in the sauna, they had plenty of opportunity for exchanging news. Carrie wore a white towel around her essentials and sat on the lower bench. Sydney wore nothing and sat on the upper.

'How'd it go then?'

'Pardon?'

'Last night.'

'Fine.'

'Yeah?'

'Yes.' Carrie cleared her throat. 'I mean, you know how it is when you do something alone for the first time when you're accustomed to doing it with someone else . . .'

'I guess so.'

Sydney lay down flat on her back. Whenever she lifted her shoulders or her buttocks, they stuck to the wooden boards, aided by the natural glue of her body's moisture. The noise this made reminded Carrie of the sound of an emery board against a ragged nail.

'Actually,' Carrie said, grinning, 'La Fille Mal Gardée is my favourite ballet.'

'Really? You like an element of slapstick, huh?'

'I suppose I must do.'

'Myself, I prefer a tragedy. I find that tragedy best reflects my emotional and psychological state.'

Carrie turned and stared straight into Heinz's frogspawn eyes. 'You're kidding.'

'Me? Kidding? Not at all. Not at all.'

24

Heinz offered Carrie his family-size box of Maltesers. 'Thanks.'

Carrie took one and popped it into her mouth. 'That's the strangest part . . .' she said, chewing and enjoying the sensation of chocolate and malt on her tongue. 'I've been to four ballets with you and never for a moment did I think you seemed like a sad or a dissatisfied person.'

It was the interval. Heinz and Carrie were propping up the theatre bar. Heinz had discovered that Carrie's favourite winter tipple was port and lemon. He'd taken to ordering her one before the show. This meant they didn't have to wait to be served during the intermission.

Heinz smiled at Carrie. 'You see the best in everyone.'

'Maybe I'm just insensitive.'

'You? Insensitive? Never. You're an angel.'

A man standing just to Carrie's left turned and stared at them. Carrie caught his eye. His expression was a mixture of amusement and confusion. Carrie took a sip of her drink. People were so funny, the way they stared. Their quizzical expressions. It had begun to dawn on her that when she was out with Heinz she became a puzzle. She became mysterious.

Alone, at home, in life, she felt like something dried-up, wrung-out and innocuous. Out with Heinz, she felt like she was transformed into something much less explicable.

Heinz was bossy and opinionated but he wasn't entirely unobservant. He rolled his eyes at Carrie. 'Probably thinks you're my daughter.'

Carrie shrugged. 'And I could be too, easily.'

Carrie often found Heinz to be genuinely perceptive.

At their second ballet together he'd said, 'And your husband . . . ?'

To which she'd responded, 'I don't ever want to talk about him.'

'Very well.'

And they'd never spoken about him since. It was almost like, Carrie decided, Jack had never even existed.

Sydney was plaiting her hair, trying, but failing, to include the front bang-like bits into the weave so that they didn't keep falling into her eyes. Their class was due to start at any minute. Carrie stood behind her, scowling to herself, intensely discomfited.

'I was only saying,' Sydney observed, still plaiting, 'that it seems a bit strange for you not to want me to come with you when you said yourself on several occasions that there was a spare ticket going begging.'

'There is a spare ticket,' Carrie said, caught distinctly off her guard. 'It's only that next week I promised someone else . . .'

'Who?'

'A friend called Sue,' Carrie said, too quickly, and then widened her eyes when she'd finished speaking as if the words she'd just uttered were indigestible.

'Who?'

'I told you about her, surely? She's the one who thinks I should open my own interior design shop.'

'Sue?'

'Yes. Remember? I said I was thinking about starting work again, now that Jack's gone. The money's tight and everything.'

'Interior design? That's the first I've heard of it. How

could you afford to open an interior design shop? You don't know anything about retail . . .'

Sydney finished her plaiting and turned to face Carrie. Carrie's cheeks were red, she noted, and she was scratching her neck as though she'd been bitten.

'It was just an idea.'

'Where would you get the money from to start a business with? You're broke.'

'I know.'

'Interior design, you said?'

Carrie nodded.

'Sue? Sue who?'

Carrie blinked and then swallowed. 'The Sue who's coming to the ballet with me next week. We were at school together. I surely must've mentioned her before.'

'No.'

People had started to filter their way gradually into the gym. Carrie pointed, 'I think the class is due to start.'

'OK, next time.'

'Pardon?'

Sydney smiled. 'Next time I want to come with you, so make sure you keep the ticket spare, all right?'

'Yes. Fine.'

Sydney led the way. Carrie looked down at her trainers and silently incanted a Hail Mary.

They'd become so engrossed in their conversation that they hadn't noticed everyone else going back inside. Carrie was so engrossed in what Heinz was saying that she almost hadn't noticed his hand on her shoulder. Almost.

'What else do I have to spend my money on? Huh? There's nothing. I want for nothing. It would give me enormous pleasure to help you out.'

'I don't know.' Carrie, for some reason, couldn't stop thinking about Sydney.

'Actually, Heinz, next time I come to the ballet I'll be bringing someone with me . . .'

Heinz's hand slipped from Carrie's shoulder. His voice was suddenly flat. 'Oh. That's good. It seems such a shame to waste the seat every week like you do.'

'Exactly. We go to the same evening class together.'

'Does this person have a name?'

'Sydney.'

'I see. I see.'

Carrie noticed that Heinz's face was pale and doughy. 'Is something wrong?'

'Nothing at all. Nothing.'

Carrie continued to stare at Heinz. Was he all right? He didn't look it. She suddenly became nervous and she didn't know why. She started to babble. 'She's Australian. I had to invite her. She asked.'

Heinz put his hand to his bow tie. 'She's a girl?'

'Yes.'

Carrie watched with ill-concealed amazement as Heinz burst out laughing. He laughed so hard and loud that his toupee slipped. Then he plucked it from his forehead with his meaty hand, tossed it into the air with a great whoop and then caught it, just as deftly.

The sauna. Sydney sat bolt upright, her eyes as wide as saucers, each hand enfolding a single breast as though her amazement endangered them in some way.

'You're sleeping with this guy?'

Carrie's towel was wrapped as tight as it could be but still she hitched it closer. 'Not exactly. I didn't spend the night . . .'

'You fucked this man?'

'Please! He's eighty-three!'

'Exactly! He's eighty-fucking-three and you shagged him. My God! How did this happen? How does it happen that an attractive forty-four-year-old woman, in her prime, great body, big hair, the lot, shags an eighty-three-year-old man who she was the first to admit . . .'

'It wasn't . . .'

'Who she was the *first* to admit is the fattest and most boring old loudmouth in the whole damn universe. How? Huh?'

'Sydney! *Please* . . .'

'Jesus, I can just imagine it.'

'Imagine what?'

'You know what I mean.'

'Don't!'

'Guess what I'm visualizing, Carrie. I am visualizing this grey slug of a man with an enormous pale belly and a tiny penis like a party-time Mars Bar hanging down below . . .'

'Stop it!'

Carrie was on the brink of crying. She was so ashamed. It wasn't even the act, the fact of it, that shamed her, only Sydney's perception of it and then *her* perception of it as a result of Sydney's. That was all. And if Sydney hadn't insisted on the second ballet ticket it would never have been a problem, she could have hidden it. She could have pretended . . .

'He must be loaded.'

'What?'

'Money. Why else would you want him? Is he loaded? Is he going to, maybe, give you a little bit of money to start off your interior design business? Is that it?'

Carrie was mortified. 'It isn't like that at all!'

'No? How is it then?'

'I don't know!' Carrie started crying.

Sydney was unmoved. She said softly, 'You know, I kept thinking you were taking this whole Jack thing too well.'

'I don't want to talk about Jack!'

'What would Jack think, huh? What would Jack actually think if he knew what you were doing?'

Carrie stood up, covered her cheeks with her hands, bolted out of the sauna, through the changing rooms and into the showers. There she turned the tap to cold, ripped off her towel and pushed her burning face into the jet.

Sydney crossed her llama legs at the knee and then dialled Jack's number.

'Hi Jack. It's Sydney.'

'Sydney? Well, hello. What can I do for you?'

'I want to see you. It's about Carrie.'

After Jack had put down the phone, he picked up his duffel coat and brushed it off. He was keenly looking forward to a cold snap.

It was a nightmare. Just as she'd imagined. Heinz wore his toupee and his turd-coloured tie. He kept regaling them with terrible stories about his late wife's beloved red setter which had died – following several years of chronic incontinence – after swallowing a cricket ball. Carrie supposed that he must be nervous. Poor lamb.

Sydney was horribly polite. She kept staring at Heinz's stomach as she spoke to him, like she expected, at any minute, that something might explode out of it.

When Carrie drove her home, she didn't talk for the

first ten minutes of the journey. She merely said, 'Carrie. Leave me. I have to *digest.*'

Carrie left her. Eventually, after she'd digested sufficiently, Sydney said, 'He belched throughout the ballet. It was like sitting next to an old pair of bellows. Christ, the orchestra should recruit him for the wind section.'

Carrie's heart sank. 'He wasn't belching. He swallowed a toffee too quickly. It went down the wrong way. He kept apologizing.'

'And that fucking dog! His dead wife's dead fucking dog! Does he really think I'm interested in how they fed it a diet of fresh chicken to try and quell its chronic flatulence? Are *you* interested, Carrie? Huh?'

'No.'

'Pardon?'

'No! No, I'm not interested. I'm not.'

'And I just can't believe . . .'

'What?' Carrie tried to keep her eyes on the road, but Sydney's expression . . . 'What?!'

'The two of you . . .'

'What?'

Sydney's eyes were glued to the road ahead. It was starting to rain. Carrie turned on the windscreen wipers just in time with Sydney's next pronouncement.

'Fucking.'

Carrie said nothing. They both stared at the road. Eventually Sydney turned her eyes towards Carrie. 'Well?'

Carrie said nothing. She focused on the road and the wipers and the rain and the way that the light from the streetlamps reflected in the drops of water on the windscreen before each harsh stroke brushed it away. Where do they go? She wondered. Where do those moments go? The rain falling in just such a way, the light, the wiper. Something there and then something gone.

Sydney found she was boiling. Not hot, but something *inside*. What else could she do? What else could she say? Carrie had closed down, shut up, like a clam. Sydney cursed herself. She was too impetuous. Too quick to judge. If only she'd tried to be nice, to be supportive. Maybe then Carrie might have provided her with some details. Something to ponder, to mull over, fat to chew on. Damn! Sydney crossed her arms, stared at the road, *boiled*.

'I got your number from the book,' Heinz said.

'Didn't I give it you?'

'No.'

'I should've.'

'She didn't like me.'

'No. Actually, I think she really hated you.'

'Sometimes I can be overwhelming. It's a fault of mine. I know that. But I am simply myself. When you get old . . .'

'You tried your best.'

'But did I? One tends to forget how it is to . . . uh . . . to play the game.'

'Never mind.'

'Can I see you?'

'Pardon?'

'Tonight?'

Carrie rubbed her eyes with her spare hand. 'I only just got in. It's raining outside . . .'

'Tomorrow?'

Sydney lay on her stomach and rested the weight of her head on her hands. What was wrong? It was just . . . she couldn't imagine. Carrie and that fat old man. My God! She just couldn't *picture* it. Not properly. Not graphically. She rolled on to her back. Couldn't imagine. But my Lord, *my Lord*, how she longed to!

Sydney stared at Jack's buttons. Jack pretended not to notice. Sydney sighed.

'Jack,' she said, 'you haven't a hope in hell of winning me over with that old three button trick.'

Jack's eyes blinked and then widened. 'What do you mean, ma'am?'

'Nor that Courtly American Gentleman shite.'

Jack scowled. 'What's the axe you've got to grind, Sydney?' he asked, not charming any longer.

'No axe,' Sydney said. 'I just thought you should know . . .' She paused. What did she want to say, exactly? Would she tell Jack about Heinz? She looked into Jack's face and knew that the notion of an eighty-odd-year-old man sleeping with his wife was hardly going to incite him to jealousy.

'Is it Carrie?' Jack asked.

'Yep.' Sydney rubbed the corner of her eyes.

'You look washed out,' he said.

'Tired. Haven't been sleeping.'

'Really?'

Sydney uncrossed her legs. 'Carrie's got someone new.'

Jack looked surprised. 'Already?'

'Yeah.'

'Who?'

Sydney cleared her throat. 'Someone she's known for a while.'

'She met them at the gym? Who is it? Do I know them?'

Sydney shrugged. 'That's not the point.'

'So I do know them?'

'I didn't say you knew them.'

'Are they younger than me?'

Sydney squirmed. 'I just thought . . .'

'Why are you telling me this?'

Sydney picked up her briefcase. 'Not for any reason, really.' She frowned and then asked out loud. 'Why am I telling you? I don't know.' She stood up. 'That three button thing you do,' she said finally, 'I just wanted to tell you that it's a real cheap trick.'

Half a bottle of Jim Beam later, it finally clicked. The only thing that made sense. Carrie was having an affair with Sydney. And Sydney was terrified of what exactly his response might be. She was intimidated by him. She was *threatened*. Naturally. And she'd really wanted to tell him too, to throw it in his face, debilitate him. Only then . . . only then she just didn't have the nerve. That was it! Had to be. Carrie and Sydney. Sydney and Carrie. Wow.

'You won't believe this, Sydney. Something so odd happened . . .' They were pulling on their leotards and tying up their laces.

'Try me.'

'Jack rang. He left a message on the machine. He wants to drop by. On Wednesday.'

Sydney pulled the bow stiff on her lace. She straightened up.

'But Wednesday!' she exclaimed. 'Isn't that ballet night?'

Carrie looked uneasy, momentarily, like she didn't know quite what Sydney was getting at. 'Uh, yes . . .'

'So you won't be needing your tickets?'

'I suppose not, unless . . .'

'So I could have them both, maybe?'

'You?'

'Yeah. I quite got a taste for it the other night. How about it, huh?'

Heinz started when he saw her. He wondered whether Carrie had come with her but had popped to the Ladies for some reason, or to the bar. He squeezed his way over to his seat.

'Hello there.'

Sydney looked up. 'Oh, hi. How are you?'

'Not too bad. Not too bad at all.'

He sat down, adjusted his position, pulled at his little bow tie which constricted him, reached into his jacket pocket and pulled from its depths a Cadbury's Chocolate Orange. He unwrapped the foil and offered the orange to Sydney.

'Dark chocolate,' he said.

Sydney tried to pull off a slice but it wouldn't come loose. Heinz intervened, knocked at the chocolate orange with the centre of his palm and then offered it her again.

'Thanks,' Sydney said, smiling, showing him what fine, straight teeth she had and just how sweet and obliging she could be.

Jack had brought flowers. Lilies. Her favourites.

'Look, Carrie, I met up with Sydney the other day.'

Carrie was putting the flowers in water, but preparing each stem first by slicing an inch off the bottom at a sharp angle. That way, she knew, the flower could drink so much more.

'Sydney?'

'Yeah.'

'She didn't mention it.'

'No?'

Jack was actually relieved. He'd been worried in case Sydney might have blotted his copybook with Carrie by suggesting things about him, by exaggerating or maligning. Sydney could bitch with the best when she felt the urge. She was dangerous.

'Let me tell you something,' Jack said, leaning his back up against one of the kitchen cupboards.

'What?' Carrie was wide-eyed and restless. What had Sydney said? Had she been indiscreet? Had she mentioned Heinz?

'I know what's been going on,' Jack said, 'and I'm here to tell you that I don't care. I've given it some thought . . .'

'What do you know?'

'About you and Sydney.'

'What about us?'

He put out both his hands. 'Just tell me,' he said, 'that it's over. Because my suitcase,' he couldn't hide his smile, 'my suitcase, darling, is lying packed in the boot of my car.'

'I'll tell you something else,' Sydney said, lounging on Heinz's sofa and drinking her fourth martini.

'What?'

Heinz was sitting on his comfy chair sipping a cup of tea.

'I went and saw Jack the other day, right? A private *tête à tête*, and he came into the café where we'd arranged to meet with the buttons on his coat done up all . . .' Sydney made a higgledy-piggledy movement with her hands, 'like so . . .'

'He's missing her?' Heinz interjected, almost sympathetic.

'No. Not at all. That's my point. It's the three button trick.'

'The what?'

'Men do it. Some men. To make them look . . .' she burped, 'vul-ner-a-ble. And this is the best bit . . .' She put her hand over her mouth. 'Pardon me.'

'The best bit?'

'Yeah. Turns out, he only pulled that trick the very first time he ever spoke to Carrie. 1972. Outside the National Portrait Gallery. Took her in completely. Beguiled her, absolutely. And there he was, large as life, trying it on with me!'

'Did you tell her?'

Sydney knocked back the rest of her drink. 'Who?'

'Carrie.'

'Nope. Seemed a shame.'

Heinz nodded.

'Nice flat,' Sydney said, looking around her.

'It suits me well enough.'

'Come and sit over here.' Sydney patted the sofa to her left. 'Come on.'

Heinz smiled. 'I am perfectly comfortable where I am, thank you.'

Sydney stared at him, balefully. 'What's wrong?'

Outside the sound of a faint car horn was just audible.

'Nothing is wrong,' Heinz said, pushing his great bulk up from his comfy chair and walking over to the window. While his back was turned, Sydney unbuttoned the grey silk shirt she was wearing and took it off. Heinz turned and said, 'I think that's your cab.'

'Huh?'

'Outside.'

'What cab?'

'I called for one a little while back.'

'A cab? Can't I stay here?'

'What for?'

Sydney started grinning but only half her mouth worked properly. 'Sex, stupid.'

Heinz picked up Sydney's pale silk shirt from the arm of the sofa and handed it to her. 'I'm eighty-three years old,' he said gently, 'and entirely impotent.'

'What's wrong?' Carrie asked, for the umpteenth time. 'I can tell something's bothering you. I only wish you'd tell me.'

Sydney had still not yet quite recovered. It was Thursday night at the gym.

'Nothing's wrong.'

She hadn't been sleeping. Her elbows were hurting. She couldn't stop thinking . . .

'I only got out of the house tonight because Jack's at a conference. I swore not to come here any more. He seems to have got the idea into his head that you're some kind of . . .' Carrie couldn't think of the appropriate word.

Sydney was staring at Carrie with an odd expression. Either Carrie lied, she was thinking, or Heinz lied.

'So Jack doesn't know about Heinz yet?'

'No.'

'Well, let's just hope he doesn't get to find out, either.'

Carrie shook her head. 'I spoke to Heinz on the phone. I explained that I didn't want Jack knowing. He was so good about it.'

'Knowing what?'

'Knowing anything.'

38

Sydney smiled at this, and Carrie, for some reason, had cause, she sensed, to feel a sudden dart of disquiet. In her stomach. In her gut.

'I told you not to ring me!' Carrie exclaimed, terrified at the possibility of discovery.

'Is it safe to talk?'

'Jack's in the bath. He's listening to the cricket on the radio.'

'You know I miss you terribly. You know that, don't you?'

'Heinz, there's no point . . .'

'But this isn't about that. It is about your friend, Sydney.'

'What?'

'She keeps calling around and she also keeps writing to me. She phones me . . .'

'Sydney?'

'I just want you to talk to her. I simply want her to leave me in peace.'

'My God. How odd.'

'I miss you so much.'

Carrie's cheeks glowed an unnaturally bright colour as she said goodbye and then gently placed down the receiver.

She waited until the last person had left the sauna. 'Carrie,' she said, 'I've done something I think you should know about.'

'What?'

'I had sex with Heinz.' She'd expected Carrie to blush or blanch. One or the other.

'What happened?'

39

'Straight sex. Nothing fancy.'

Carrie frowned, 'I'm afraid I don't believe you, Sydney.'

'Why not? It's true.'

'He's impotent.'

'He isn't. You slept with him.'

'I didn't sleep with him.'

'You said you did.'

'He's impotent.'

'So what . . .'

'He's in love with me. He'll do *anything*.'

Sydney stared at Carrie, confounded. Carrie was round and soft and lily white. She seemed peculiarly full of herself.

'So let me get this straight . . .' Sydney said, wanting details so badly.

'He just wants you to leave him in peace.'

'Does Jack know yet?' Sydney asked, knowing she was routed and turning nasty.

'He doesn't know.'

Carrie appeared unperturbed. Sydney shrugged. 'Better make sure he doesn't find out, then.'

Carrie only smiled.

'Jack made a move on me, when we met up recently,' Sydney said. 'He tried that old three button trick of his.'

'What do you mean?'

'So you don't even know about that one yet?' Sydney asked. 'Oh, you'll just love it. It's so cheap.' And she set about putting Carrie straight on that particular matter.

He'd kept on nagging so in the end she'd been forced to give in to him. 'It's a terrible waste,' he said, 'to keep on leaving the seats empty.'

Anyhow, Carrie was bored of sitting at home every night with nothing to do and no proper conversation. Sometimes he mentioned the name of a new actress. Sometimes he wasn't too tactful and inadvertently made her feel her age.

When Heinz finally entered the box, a little late, without his tie, pale-faced, dishevelled, Jack muttered, 'Christ, I'd almost forgotten about him.'

Carrie said nothing, but she hadn't forgotten.

Sydney was sitting on her bed and in front of her was a pile of scrap books. She opened the first one. Dry red wines from the Perth region. She touched the wine label and wondered about her mummy and her daddy. Her elbows were itchy. She reached for a tub of Vaseline. She dipped in her fingers.

Heinz had had several options: to forget about her, to confront her and tell her what a bastard Jack was, to be a kind of bastard himself. He was old. If he'd learned anything along the line, he'd learned that the little things didn't matter, at the end of the day, but the big things mattered, and sometimes you had to compromise yourself, however slightly, to try to maintain that bigger picture.

In the interval they bumped into one another at the bar. Jack was several feet away ordering drinks. Heinz had given plenty of thought to this moment. He'd had several options available. He'd taken the cheapest. Arriving late, no tie, the business.

'You look terrible,' she said, glancing over towards Jack, her lips barely moving. She stared at his shirt. 'And your buttons,' she added, 'are done up all wrong.'

He looked down at himself. 'Really?' he said, wheezing, like he'd barely noticed. But when he looked back up again his old heart began pumping.

Jack was walking over towards them holding two glasses. A whisky, a port and lemon. He was walking over. He was close and he was closer.

Carrie put out her hand and touched Heinz's buttons. 'Oh God,' she said softly, 'that stupid three button trick, you old hound,' and her eyes started sparkling.

WESLEY

Blisters

'Look,' Trevor said, 'you've got to serve from the back, see?'

Wesley dropped the orange he'd just picked up.

'Put it where it was before,' Trevor said sniffily. 'Exactly.'

Wesley adjusted the placement of the orange. There. Just so. It was neat now. The display looked hunky-dory.

'Let me quickly say something,' Wesley said, as Trevor turned to go and unload some more boxes from the van.

'What?'

'It's just that if you serve people from the back of the stall they immediately start thinking that what you're giving them isn't as good as what's on display.'

Trevor said nothing.

'See what I mean?'

'So what?'

'Well, I'm just saying that if you want to build up customer confidence then it's a better idea to give them the fruit they can see.'

'It's more work that way,' Trevor said, shoving his hands into his pockets.

'Well, I don't care about that,' Wesley responded. 'I'm the one who'll end up having to do most of the serving while you're running the deliveries and I don't mind.'

Trevor gave Wesley a deep look and then shrugged and walked off to the van.

Another new job. Selling fruit off a stall on the Roman Road. Wesley was handsome and intelligent and twenty-three years old and he'd had a run of bad luck so now he was working the markets. No references needed. Actually, on the markets a bad temper was considered something of a bonus. Nobody messed you around. If they did, though, then you had to look out for yourself.

Trevor had red hair and a pierced nose. Wesley looked very strait-laced to him in his clean corduroy trousers and polo-neck jumper, and his hands were soft and he spoke too posh. What Trevor didn't realize, however, was that Wesley had been spoilt rotten as a child so was used to getting his own way and could manipulate and wheedle like a champion if the urge took him. Wesley had yet to display to Trevor the full and somewhat questionable force of his personality.

Wesley pulled his weight. That, at least, was something, Trevor decided. After they'd packed up on their first night he invited Wesley to the pub for a drink as a sign of his good faith. Wesley said he wanted something to eat instead. So they went for pie and mash together.

Trevor had some eels and a mug of tea. Wesley ate a couple of meat pies. Wesley liked the old-fashioned tiles and the tables in the pie and mash shop. He remarked on this to Trevor. Trevor grunted.

'My dad was in the navy,' Wesley said, out of the blue.
'Yeah?'
'He taught me how to box.'
'Yeah?'
'Last job I had, I punched my boss in the face. He was up a ladder. I was on a roof. Broke his collar bone.'

'You're kidding!' Trevor was impressed.

'Nope.'

'Fuck.'

'Yeah.'

'What did he do?'

'Tried to prosecute.'

'What!?'

'I buggered off. I live my life,' Wesley said plainly, 'by certain rules. I'll do my whack, but when push comes to shove, I want to be treated decent and to keep my mind free. See?'

Trevor was mystified. He ate his eels, silently.

'I had a brother,' Wesley said, 'and I killed him when I was a kid. An accident and everything. But that's made me think about things in a different way.'

'Yeah?' Trevor was hostile now. 'How did you kill him?'

'Playing.'

'Playing what?'

'None of your fucking business.'

Trevor's eyebrows rose and he returned to his meal.

'I want to do the decent thing,' Wesley said. 'You know? And sometimes that'll get you into all kinds of grief.'

Trevor didn't say anything.

'Watch this.'

Trevor looked up. Wesley had hold of one of the meat pies. He opened his mouth as wide as he could and then pushed the pie in whole. Every last crumb. Trevor snorted. He couldn't help it. Once Wesley had swallowed the pie he asked Jean – the woman who served part-time behind the counter – for a straw. When she gave him one, he drank a whole mug of tea through it up his left nostril.

Trevor roared with laughter. He was definitely impressed.

After a week on the job Wesley started nagging Trevor

about the quality of the fruit he was buying from the wholesalers. 'The way I see it, right,' Wesley said, 'if you sell people shit they won't come back. If you sell them quality, they will.'

'Bollocks,' Trevor said, 'this ain't Marks and fucking Spencer's.'

Wesley moaned and wheedled. He told Trevor he'd take a cut in his money if Trevor spent the difference on buying better quality stuff. Eventually Trevor gave in. And he took a cut in his wages too.

After a month, Wesley used his own money to repaint the stall a bright green and bought some lights to hang on it to make it, as he said, 'more of a proposition'.

'Thing is,' Wesley observed, fingering the little string of lights, 'we have to get one of the shops to let us tap into their electricity supply, otherwise we can't use them.'

Trevor didn't really care about the lights but he was grudgingly impressed by the pride Wesley seemed to take in things. He went to the newsagents and the bakery and then finally into the pie and mash shop. Fred, who ran the shop, agreed to let them use his power if they paid him a tenner a week. Wesley said this seemed a reasonable arrangement.

Things were going well. Wesley would spend hours juggling apples for old ladies and did a trick which involved sticking the sharpened end of five or six matches between the gaps in his teeth and then lighting the matches up all at once. He'd burned his lips twice that way and had a permanent blister under the tip of his nose. He'd pick at the blister for something to do until the clear plasma covered his fingers and then he'd say, 'Useful, this, if ever I got lost in a desert. Water on tap.'

After six weeks things had reached a point where

Trevor would have done anything Wesley suggested. The stall was flourishing. Business was good. Wesley worked his whack and more so. He kept everyone amused with his tricks and his silly ideas. The customers loved him. He was always clean.

What it was that made Wesley so perfect in Trevor's eyes was the fact that he was a curious combination of immense irresponsibility – he was a mad bastard – and enormous conscientiousness. He wanted to *do* good but this didn't mean he had to *be* good.

One morning, two months after Wesley had started on the stall, Trevor got a flat tyre on his way back from the wholesalers and Wesley was obliged to set up on his own and do a couple of the early deliveries himself into the bargain.

He took Fred at the pie and mash shop his regular bundle of fresh parsley and then asked him for the extension cord so that he could put up his lights on the stall. Fred was busy serving. He indicated with his thumb towards the back of the shop. 'Help yourself, mate. The lead and everything's just behind the door. That's where Trevor stashes them each night.'

Fred liked Wesley and he trusted him. Same as Trevor did and all the others. Wesley, if he'd had any sense, should have realized that he was well set up here.

Wesley wandered out to the rear of the shop. He pulled back the door and picked up the extension lead. Then he paused. It was cold. He looked around him.

A big room. Red, polished, concrete floors. Large, silver fridges. And quiet. He could hear the noise from the shop and, further off, the noise from the market. But in here it was still and the stillness and the silence had a special *sound*. Like water.

Wesley closed his eyes. He shuddered. He opened his eyes again, tucked the lead under his arm and beat a hasty retreat.

He was in a world of his own when Trevor finally arrived that morning. On two occasions Trevor said, 'Penny for them,' and then snapped his fingers in front of Wesley's unfocused eyes when he didn't respond.

'I'm thinking of my dad,' Wesley said. 'Don't ask me why.'

'Why?' said Trevor, who was in a fine good-humour considering his tyre hold-up.

'I was just in the pie and mash shop getting the extension lead for the lights. Out the back. And then I was suddenly thinking about my dad. You know, the navy and the sea and all the stuff we used to talk about when I was a kid.'

'Your dad still in the navy?' Trevor asked.

Wesley shook his head. 'Desk job,' he said.

'Probably those bloody eels,' Trevor said, bending down and picking up a crate of Coxes.

'What?'

'Those eels out the back. Making you think of the sea.'

'What?'

'In the fridges. He keeps the eels in there.'

'How's that?' Wesley's voice dipped by half an octave. Trevor didn't notice. He was wondering whether he could interest Wesley in selling flowers every Sunday as a side-interest. A stall was up for grabs on the Mile End Road close to the tube station. Sundays only.

'You're telling me he keeps live eels in those fridges?'

'What?'

'Live eels?' Wesley asked, with emphasis.

'In the fridges, yeah.' Trevor stopped what he was

doing, straightened up, warned by the tone of Wesley's voice.

'What, like . . .' Wesley said, breathing deeply, 'swimming around in a big tank?'

'Nope.' Trevor scratched his head. 'Uh . . . like five or six long metal drawers, horizontal, yeah? And when you pull the drawers open they're all in there. Noses at one end and tails at the other. Big fuckers, though. I mean, five foot each or something.'

A woman came up to the stall and wanted to buy a lemon and two bananas. She asked Wesley for what she needed but Wesley paid her no heed.

'Hang on a second,' he said gruffly, holding up his flat hand, 'just shut up for a minute.'

He turned to Trevor. 'You know anything about eels?' he asked. Trevor knew enough about wild creatures to know that if Wesley had been a dog or a coyote his ears would be prickling, his ruff swelling.

'Not to speak of . . .' he said.

'Excuse me.' Wesley said to the customer, 'I'll be back in a minute,' and off he went.

Wesley strolled into the pie and mash shop. Fred was serving. Wesley waited patiently in line until it was his turn to be served.

'What can I get you, Wesley?' Fred asked, all jovial.

Wesley smiled back at him. 'Having a few problems with the lights on the stall,' he said. 'Could I just pop out the back and see if the plug's come loose or something?'

'Surely,' Fred said, thumbing over his shoulder. 'You know the lie of the land out there.'

Wesley went into the back room and up to one of the fridges. He took hold of the top drawer and pulled it open.

The drawer contained water, and, just as Trevor had described, was crammed full of large, grey eels, all wriggling, eyes open, noses touching steel, tails touching steel. Skin rubbing skin rubbing skin.

Held in limbo, Wesley thought, in this black, dark space. Wanting to move. Wanting to move. Wanting to move. Nowhere to go. Like prison. Like purgatory.

Wesley closed the drawer. He shuddered. He covered his face with his soft hands. He breathed deeply. He hadn't been all that honest. What he'd said about his dad and everything. True enough, his dad had been in the navy, he'd travelled on ships the world over, to India and Egypt and Hong Kong. Only he never came back from the sea. Never came back home. Sort of lost interest in them all. Only sent a card once, a while after . . . a while after . . . to say he wouldn't ever be back again.

Wesley knew all about the sea, though. Knew all about fishes and currents and stingrays and everything. His mum had bought him a book about it. For his birthday when he was six. And so he knew about eels and how they all travelled from that one special place in the Sargasso Sea. Near the West Indies. That's where they were spawned and that's where they returned to die.

But first, such a journey! Feeding on plankton, the tiny, little transparent eels, newborn, floated to the surface of that great sea from their deep, warm home in its depths, drifted on the Gulf Stream, travelled over the Atlantic, for three summers, then into European waters, in huge numbers, swam upriver, from salt to freshwater. What a journey. And man couldn't tame them or breed them in captivity or stop them. Couldn't do it.

How did they know? Huh? Where to go? How did they know? But they knew! They knew where to go.

Moving on, living, knowing, remembering. Something *in* them. Something inside. Passed down through the generations. An instinct.

Wesley uncovered his face and looked around him. He wanted to find another exit. He walked to the rear of the fridges and discovered a door, bolted. He went over and unbolted it, turned the key that had been left in its lock, came back around the fridges and strolled out into the shop.

'Thanks, mate,' Wesley said as he pushed his way past Fred and sauntered back outside again.

Trevor shook his head. 'No way,' he said. And he meant it.

'You've got to fucking do this for me, Trev,' Wesley said.

'Why?'

'You know how old some of those eels are?'

'No.'

'Some could be twenty years old. They've lived almost as long as you have.'

'They get them from a farm,' Trevor said. 'They aren't as old as all that.'

'They can't breed them in captivity,' Wesley said. 'They come from the Sargasso Sea. That's where they go to breed and to die.'

'The what?'

'Near the West Indies. That's where they go. That's what eels do. They travel thousands of miles to get here and then they grow and then they travel thousands of miles to get back again.'

'Sounds a bit bloody stupid,' Trevor said, 'if you ask me.'

'I'm a travelling man,' Wesley said, 'like my dad was.

Don't try and keep me in one place. Don't try and lock me away.'

'They're eels, Wesley,' Trevor said, almost losing patience.

'Imagine how they're feeling,' Wesley said, 'caught in those fridges. Needing to travel. Needing it, needing it. Like an illness, almost. Like a fever. Dreaming of those hot waters, the deep ocean. Feeling cold steel on their noses, barely breathing, crammed together. Nowhere to go. No-fucking-where to go.'

'Forget it,' Trevor said, 'I've got no argument with Fred. Forget it, mate.'

'Take the van, Trevor,' Wesley said calmly. 'Drive it round the back, where they make the deliveries. I already unlocked the door.'

Off Wesley strode again. Trevor jangled the keys in his pocket, swore out loud and then ran after him.

Wesley crept in through the back entrance. He stood still a while. He could hear the chattering of customers in the shop and he could hear the sound of a van pulling into the delivery passage. He went outside, smiling wildly, happy to be fucking up, same as he always was.

'OK, Trev,' he said. 'Open the back doors but keep the tail up so's when I dump them in there they don't escape.'

Trevor looked immensely truculent but he did as Wesley asked.

Wesley went back inside, opened up one of the big, silver drawers, pushed his arms in, down and under all that silky, scaleless eel-flesh. He curled his arms right under, five eels, all wriggling, closed his arms around them and lifted. Water splashed and splattered. He looked over to the doorway leading into the shop, bit his lip, couldn't pause. The eels were whipping and lashing and swerving and writhing. He headed for the exit at top speed.

Trevor stood by the tailgate. When he saw the eels he swore. 'Fuck this man! Fuck this.'

Wesley threw the eels into the back of the van. 'Ten minutes,' he said, 'to get them back to water, otherwise they'll suffocate.'

Trevor watched the eels speeding and curling in the back of his van, swimming, almost, on air. He turned to say something but Wesley was gone. A minute later Wesley re-emerged. More eels. Like snakes. Faces like . . . faces like cats or otters or something. Little gills. Seal eyes.

As Wesley turned to go back in Trevor caught him by his shirt sleeve. 'I'm not doing this,' he said. 'Things are going well for us here. He's kept eels in this place for years, gets a delivery every week.'

Wesley turned on him. 'Give me the keys.'

'What?'

'Give me the shitting keys and I'll drive them to the canal myself.'

'This is stupid!'

'Don't call me fucking stupid. No one calls me that. Give me the fucking keys.'

Trevor took the keys out of his pocket and dropped them on the floor. He walked off. His eyes were prickling. 'Fuck it!' he shouted, and his voice echoed down the passageway.

Back inside, Wesley pulled open the third drawer, shoved his arms in, took hold of the eels. Water was everywhere now. Thank God it was lunchtime and Fred was busy. He held the fish tight and straightened up. He headed for the back door.

Outside, he met Fred. He was holding the five eels. He looked at Fred.

'What the hell are you doing?' Fred said.

'Why aren't you in the shop?' Wesley asked, stupidly.

'Jean's in,' Fred said, eyeing the eels. 'She's covering.'

'Oh. I didn't know that.'

'What are you doing with my eels?' Fred put out his arms. 'Give them to me.'

'No,' Wesley said. 'You can't own a wild thing.'

As he spoke he took a step back. Fred moved forwards and put himself between Wesley and the tailgate. The eels were itching to get free. Wesley's arms were aching. Fred took a step closer. He was short and square and tough as a boxing hare.

Wesley opened his arms. The eels flew into the air, landed, skidded, flipped, whipped, scissored, dashed. At top speed, they sea-snaked down the passageway, into the market, on to the main road.

'Down the Roman Road,' Wesley yelled. 'Back to the water, back to the frigging sea!'

Fred punched Wesley in the mouth. Jesus, Wesley thought, feels like all my teeth have shifted. He staggered, righted himself, clenched his hands into fists, by way of a diversion, then kicked Fred in the bollocks. Fred buckled.

Wesley skipped past him and sprang into the van. Got the keys in the ignition, started the engine, roared off in a cloud of black exhaust fume.

Beale's Place, Wright's Road, St Stephen's Road. Bollocks to the One Way! Sharp right at the tip of the market. Back on to the Roman Road, screw the traffic, on to the pavement, over the zebra crossing, past the video shop, the church, the intersection, Mile End Park. Sharp left. Over the grass. Tyre tracks. Mud-cut. Foot flat. Brakes.

How long had he taken? He didn't know. He could see the canal, just below. Dirty, dark waters. Dank and littery.

Down with the tailgate! The eels were like flying fish. The air made them pump and shudder. Like spaghetti in a heated pan, boiling and bubbling.

'Get in there!' Wesley yelled at them. 'The Grand Union Canal, the Thames, the Channel, the Ant-bloody-arctic.'

A cluster of eels shuddered down into the grass, rippled on to the concrete path, and then One! Two! Three! Four! Five! Six! Seven! Eight! Into the canal.

One eel split from the others, turned right and darted towards some undergrowth. One stayed in the back of the van, smaller than the others and less agile. Wesley grabbed it by its tail. He swung it in his arms. He ran to the edge of the canal. He threw it. The eel made a whip-cracking motion in the air, shaped itself like a fancy ribbon, just untied from a box of something wrapped and precious. Then splosh! It was under.

Wesley stood by the canal for several minutes. He inspected his hands, he sniffed, he stopped shaking. He started walking. He walked. He walked. He passed by a fisherman. He stopped walking. He looked over his shoulder. 'Which way is it to the sea?' he asked casually. 'From here, I mean?'

The fisherman gave this question some consideration while sucking his tongue and rolling his rod between his two hands.

'I should think,' he said, eventually, 'I should think it's in the exact opposite direction from the one you're travel-ling.' Then he turned, stared down along the path Wesley had just trodden, and pointed.

Braces

After she'd eaten her sandwiches, Joy would push her hand into her mouth, manipulate her fingers – Wesley could hear the clink as her short nails touched steel – and grunt and puff as she laboriously pulled her braces out. She'd had problems with her top row ever since she'd lost her first set of milk teeth. The main front incisor was buckled and protrusive, had a gap to its left but partially covered its neighbour to the right.

To rectify this problem, a dentist had fitted Joy with a thin wire which circled her front teeth and was held in place by a large, plastic disc.

This disc had been specifically modelled to the contours of the roof of Joy's mouth. Not modelled well enough, though, by every indication, because bits of bread and fruit and food and sweet-stuff always got lodged under it while she ate. They snook and snuck and jostled against the wire and the roof of her mouth. They stuck around and niggled her, even after gargling.

Wesley watched as Joy sucked her teeth and then inspected the brace as it lay on her hand. It was semi-transparent. It made him think of jelly fish and the middle of an oyster. 'Ruff! Ruff!' he barked, and bounced around like a dog so that he didn't have to watch her as she picked at the residue on her brace with her fingers and then licked them clean with her tongue. It was like she was eating a second meal, he thought, feeling intimate twinges in his gut.

Joy, distracted from her brace by Wesley's barking, glanced over at him. 'Shut up, big mouth!' she yelled, and then, 'Crunchy peanut butter!' she glowered. 'Tell your mum to buy smooth next time. It's easier.'

Wesley stopped bouncing and barking. He stood perfectly still, like she'd asked, and nodded submissively. 'Will do,' he said.

Wesley had invented a series of rules for himself. He was nine years old and had a terrible strawberry-coloured nerve rash on his right cheek which he'd had for so long that even his mother acted like it was a birthmark and told the people at his new school – his teacher, the dinner ladies – that it was simply something he was born with.

His mother let him do just as he pleased. If he wanted sweets she would give him some money. If he wanted a gun or a sword or a portable television she would buy it for him. She didn't like Joy, but she couldn't stop him from seeing her. She wouldn't dare, she wouldn't.

Wesley was so busy and there were so many things to do. Joy would come with him. She was a little bit older than him and she had a bad temper. Sometimes she tripped him up or spat at him and often she gave him Chinese burns.

'Stupid, stupid boy! Stupid boy!'

There were several children at his new school who asked him to play with them, but Joy told him that they were ignorant. 'They don't know,' she'd say, 'all the things we know.' And then she'd tell him to do something naughty as a dare and he'd do it because otherwise, Joy told him, he would break his arm or his mum would be in a car accident.

Joy was so pretty. She wore her yellow hair in a pony tail and she had blisters on her ankles and bruises on her knees.

One of his new friends at school was called Simon. Simon liked to play basketball and he could walk on his hands. Wesley liked Simon and even asked his mother to buy him a basketball jacket like the one Simon wore. Joy didn't like Simon, though, and she didn't like basketball.

'There's a new rule, Wesley,' she said, as they walked home from school one afternoon. 'If you play with Simon again then I'll hit you in the face. Like this.' Joy hit Wesley in the face. 'See?'

Wesley nodded. He touched his cheek where it stung.

'Good.' Joy smiled. She was happy again.

Wesley's mother was angry about the jacket. He brought it home and it was ripped and muddy. She held it up and inspected it.

'What happened, Wesley?'

Wesley didn't want to get Joy into trouble. He said nothing.

'Did someone at school do this to your jacket?'

He nodded.

'Who?'

He shrugged.

It was half past ten and Wesley's mother was walking past Wesley's bedroom. He'd been in bed for almost an hour and he should have been asleep by now. She stood outside his door and listened. It sounded as though Wesley was clapping his hands. Clap! Clap! Clap!

She pushed his door ajar and peered inside. Wesley was sitting up in bed and he was slapping his own face. Slapping his cheek. Slap, slap, slap! His eyes were blank as she approached but his cheeks were wet with tears. She caught hold of his hand. She kissed it. 'Lie down,' she whispered, and later, once he was sleeping, 'I love you.'

The week before the end of term, Wesley's mother had been called to the school to speak to Wesley's teacher. Wesley had attacked one of the other children with a broken tree branch. The boy was called Simon and could walk on his hands. Wesley had attacked him while he was performing this trick and had knocked him over and then hit him in the face with the broken branch. He had grazed his hands and his face was scratched.

Wesley's mother was embarrassed and confused and concerned and she didn't quite know what to do. Eventually she said, 'I thought Wesley and Simon were friends . . .'

The teacher nodded. 'They were a while ago but lately Wesley has become rather withdrawn.'

Wesley's mother scratched her forehead. 'You know, a few weeks back I bought Wesley a new basketball jacket and then he came home from school a couple of days later and it was muddy and ripped and torn. Do you think it's possible that Simon might have been bullying him?'

The teacher sighed. 'I don't know. I don't think so.'

'But it's possible?'

The teacher shrugged. 'Possible, but unlikely. About Wesley's father . . .'

'He's away at sea most of the time.'

'Maybe Wesley misses him . . . ?'

'It's not that.' Wesley's mother's face seemed to glisten under the classroom's fluorescent light. 'It's not his father he's missing.' She paused. 'It's his brother.'

The teacher put her head to one side but said nothing.

'His brother died four years ago when Wesley was five. He got shut in an old discarded refrigerator and suffocated. Wesley was out playing with him when it happened.'

'I see.'

'But he's all right now. He's a perfectly normal little boy and he knows that I'm always here for him and that I love him . . .'

'It's only five days,' Wesley told Joy, 'until the school holidays, and then we can play together all the time.'

Joy was very full of herself lately, but it seemed like the more success she had with her high-handed techniques and her bullying, the less content she felt about things.

'Wesley,' she said, picking at the blister on her ankle until white plasma squirted out of it and slid into her sock. 'You are my special friend, aren't you? You will look after me, won't you?'

'I will, I will,' Wesley said, passionately, his eyes filling.

His mother had picked him up in the car because it was the last day of school and he had some books and some drawings to take home with him.

'So, Wesley,' his mum said, 'what shall we do in the holidays? Shall we go to the cinema? Shall we go to Whipsnade Zoo?' She stopped off at their local Wimpy Bar on the way home and bought him a burger and a milkshake.

They were almost home and then Wesley became tense and distracted.

'Mum,' he said, 'we must go back.'

'Where?'

'School.'

'Why?'

'Joy. I left her in the classroom.'

'What?'

'I left Joy in the classroom. That was the last time I saw her and now she's gone.'

Wesley's mother pulled the car over to the side of the road. 'Wesley,' she said softly, 'I'm sure Joy can easily find you if she wants to.'

Wesley's eyes were wide and frightened. 'But she's in the classroom! We must get her! If she stays in the classroom she'll starve over the summer and she'll die!'

His mother smiled. 'Maybe a cleaner will go in there later and she'll get out then. Or maybe the teacher left a window open. She'll find her own way home.'

Wesley started sobbing. He was inconsolable.

Wesley's teacher met Wesley's mother in the school car park. It was eight o'clock and Wesley had been crying for four and a half hours. He was sitting in the car, still crying.

'You must think I'm a fool,' Wesley's mother said, 'but I can't stand seeing him so distressed. He's just got it into his head that his little friend is locked in the classroom and nothing I can say . . .'

The teacher looked over towards the car. Wesley's face was puce with sobbing. 'When his brother died,' she said gently, 'how did he react?'

Wesley's mother shook her head. 'Just quiet and frightened. Not a tear.'

The teacher sighed. 'This is his way of grieving for his brother,' she said. If we unlock the classroom, it'll be almost like we're pretending that we can bring his brother back. Do you know what I mean?'

Wesley's mother was scowling but she sort of understood. She said, 'Wesley makes up little games and little rules for himself all the time . . .'

'And why,' his teacher added, 'would he have decided to lock this invisible friend of his in the classroom if he hadn't wanted, in his heart of hearts, to finally be rid of her?'

The car door slammed. Wesley was out of the car and racing towards the school buildings, in the dark, towards his classroom. His mother, his teacher, called out and then followed him.

They found Wesley with his face pushed up against the window of the schoolroom. He was looking for Joy but he couldn't see her in the darkness. 'Open it!' he screamed. 'Let her out! Open it! Open it!'

And when they wouldn't open it he started slapping his face on his bad cheek. His teacher tried to hold him and his mother tried to hug him. But they wouldn't open it. His teacher kept saying, 'She's not in there. You don't need her. You lost her because you wanted to.'

And his mother kept saying, 'It's not Christopher. Christopher is dead now, Wesley. Christopher is dead now.'

Wesley broke free. He ran from them, screaming, his arms windmilling, so angry that they'd mentioned Christopher, so angry that Joy was stuck in the classroom and they wouldn't let him have her back. And he'd never been angry before, not really. Joy was the angry one. Joy was the cross one who made him do bad things but now

Joy was gone and he was angry. They had taken her. They had taken her. And now she would starve during the summer holidays. Oh, his throat – oh, his chest – oh, his *heart*.

Joy sat at a desk. Now what? She was bored. It was dark in here. There was nothing to do. She found some chalk and scribbled on the blackboard. She drew a big white rectangle. She stared at it for a while. 'Christopher,' she whispered, 'come and play with me. Christopher, Christopher, come and play.'

Nothing happened. She scratched at the blisters on her ankles. She closed her eyes. And then she moved herself, in an electric current, in a bolt of static, in an electrical pulse, out of that classroom and into Wesley's brain.

Wesley was still running and shouting and screaming. He was making so much noise that he didn't even know Joy had come back to him. She moved herself, her braces and her blisters and her bruises, into the darkest corner of Wesley's mind, that place where Christopher was. And they played together then, Joy and Christopher, the two of them, quietly, silently. Bitter, ugly, cruel little games which nobody knew about.

Even Wesley stopped remembering who they really were.

Mr Lippy

The first time Iris met Mr Lippy he was in Hunstanton, sitting on the ocean wall, watching the tide from the Wash as it lapped away at the concrete just below his feet. His right fist was wrapped up in a thick, white gauze. Iris guessed straight away that he must have sustained this injury in a fight. She should have avoided him. Naturally. If only she'd known what was good for her. Perhaps she didn't know. Or if she did, she didn't care.

'Hi,' she said.

'I don't talk to girls,' he responded.

'You from the West Country?' she asked, brutally, registering some kind of rural burr in his voice.

He said nothing.

'How'd you hurt your hand, then?'

He ignored her.

'Live around here?'

She sat down next to him and swung her legs. She was eighteen and liked a challenge. She wore sandals and a halter-neck top even though it was late October.

His bottom lip stuck out while she spoke to him. He pouted without thinking, like he was sulking about something, only he didn't know what, didn't know, even, that he was sulking.

'What's a good-looking man like you got to sulk about?' she said.

'Pardon?' He turned and looked at her.

'Mr Lippy!' She laughed. She stuck her bottom lip out, mimicking him.

'I wasn't doing that!'

'Wanna bet?'

'I wasn't!' He switched on his brain and stared at her properly, for the first time.

From that moment onwards, Iris always called him Mr Lippy if he scowled or sulked or swore at her. His real name was Wesley but she called him Wes. She always wanted things different from the way they were.

Wesley had yearned all his life to be close to the sea. His dad had been a sailor. But he was born inland and had lived there until he'd arrived at the Wash under his own steam aged twenty-four. Now he was twenty-eight.

Sometimes he worked on the funfair in Hunstanton. Sometimes he went potato picking. He worked in the sugar beet factory until they closed it, and then, after a spate in the arcade, got a job ferrying tourists across the Wash in an open-topped, antiquated hovercraft to visit Seal Island.

Iris didn't know that Wesley's broken fist had been sustained, not in a fight as she'd imagined, but in an accident at work: one of the other lads had reversed the hovercraft too close to the ocean wall where Wesley was stationed at the back of the craft, ready to put out the gang-plank. The lad's foot had slipped off the brake on to the accelerator, and Wesley's hand had been crushed that way.

An accident. But Wesley relished the pain. He liked punishment. And anyhow, he'd received several hundred pounds in compensation, just like that. A gift from the gods. So he opened a bank account and nested it there.

Iris was living in a bed and breakfast facing the seafront. She was a bully but he thought it was because life had been hard on her. He was wrong. They made love under a single duvet. If Wesley got carried away, if he threatened to come before she was ready, then she'd squeeze his bad fist until he saw only stars. It was good, she thought, to keep him distracted. Just a little bit.

He'd known her for a month when she told him she was pregnant. She didn't know anything about him.

'I don't care,' he said, 'what happens, really, so long as I can stay close to the sea.'

'Why?' She was only two weeks pregnant but already she felt different about things and she wanted Wesley to feel different too.

'I don't know. My dad was a sailor.'

'Really? And your mum?'

'She lives in Gloucester.'

'Yeah? Think she'll be pleased?'

Wesley shrugged. Iris waited for Wesley to ask about her mum and dad. He didn't ask. She wanted him to.

'Do you love me?'

'I'm used to being on my own.'

'Don't you have any plans? For the future, I mean?'

Wesley rearranged the gauze on his fist.

'Not me,' he said.

'Why not?'

Wesley closed his eyes.

Seal Island. In the summer the boat was packed to its gills with children. Clutching their packed lunches and their cans of fizzy pop. They'd all passed the morning on the big wheel and the dodgems, eating candy-floss and bags of sticky honeycomb. And now they were headed for Seal Island. They had dreams of palm trees and Captain Hook and hidden treasure to help them over the brown sea and the lurching waves. An island, full of basking seals.

When the tide was out, you might see the sluttish brown outline of the sandbank. You might see a lethargic seal, on its edge, rolling to the bank's perimeter, and then the flip of its tail as it swam off and under. If the tide was in, you were lucky to see that much.

Seal Island. Wesley loved it. Every day. The tears, the screams, the disappointment. He loved that stuff. He'd turn and he'd look at the children, the occasional mum, the odd uncle. And he'd think, 'Good, they should learn that life is shit. Good they should know it.'

Iris became worried about Wesley's motivation. 'That's cruel,' she'd say, 'to lead the little buggers into thinking that they're getting more for their money than they've a right to expect.'

'No crueller,' Wesley said, 'than leading them into thinking that life is anything better than a bitch.'

One day Wesley came back to Iris's room to discover her parents there. They weren't at all as he'd imagined.

'Mum and Dad want me to come home again,' Iris said, 'and I want you to come with me, Wes.'

'Home, where?' he asked, shifting his weight from foot to foot.

She'd promised him it was close to the sea. In the back of the car, they sat. One suitcase between them. 'Nearly there,' she kept saying. 'Nearly, nearly.'

Iris's father showed Wesley the shop, the nursery, the rabbit pen, the pet section, the field with the ponies, the café. The whole kit and caboodle. Finally he showed him the owl sanctuary. Twenty cages.

'What's it mean?' Wesley asked. 'Sanctuary?'

'Couldn't survive in the wild,' Iris's father said. 'Some come from exotic places.'

Wesley stared at the owls. They stared back. Not blinking.

'You never told me,' Wesley said, that night, in their bedroom, 'that your parents were rich like this.'

'Never asked,' Iris said.

'I don't understand,' Wesley said, 'why anyone should want to run away from something that's as good as here.'

Iris shrugged. 'I'm back, aren't I?' she said, all saucy.

'It's far from the sea,' Wesley said.

'Fuck that shit.'

He turned to look at her.

'You don't even like the sea,' she said, 'not really. It just makes you sad and angry. It's all mixed up in your head with some stupid fantasy about your dad.'

Wesley was injured by this. It was almost as though, he thought, Iris didn't respect his reasons. Like his reasons weren't good enough.

Big eyes. Big wings. Big beaks. He'd feed them little chicks and small white mice. Their keeper, Derek, told Wesley all about them. 'See those big eyes,' he'd say. 'Well, that leads people into thinking that they're wise and all, but they aren't.'

'No?'

'No. Their eye sockets take up much of the space in their skulls, so their brain is as tiny as a hazelnut, just about.'

Wesley would stare at the owls for hours on end,

unblinking, but only during the week. At weekends he avoided the sanctuary because then it was crowded with tourists who whistled and screamed and pointed. Some of the cages had little notices which read: MIND FINGERS AND NOSES. THESE ARE WILD ANIMALS. DO NOT TOUCH WIRE MESH.

Wesley worked in the nursery. Sometimes he helped out in the cafeteria. Iris would trail around after him, trying to make him smile.

'Aren't you happy here?' she'd ask. 'Don't you love me?'

He did quite like her, actually.

'Do you resent me being pregnant?'

'Nope.'

'Will we ring your mother yet and tell her about it?'

'Nope.'

'Why not? Why *not*?' It had started to gall Iris, his inability to celebrate *anything*.

One owl especially. He'd stare and stare. It was as big as a spaniel. Grey feathered. Pop-eyed, crazy-looking. Like an emu. Like something unimaginable.

Wesley wondered what would happen if he set the bird free. When he was younger he'd dreamed about freedom, but now he was resigned to a life of drudgery. Free, he'd whisper, and then, die. Free. Die. Free. Die. Free. Die.

Derek had told him, you see, that if the owls were released they would starve to death or some of them would freeze. They were too bloody conspicuous, Wesley thought, for their own safety.

'Why don't you want me to meet your family? Are you ashamed of me? Am I too young?'

Wesley stood up, picked up his coat, as if to leave the room.

'Where are you going?'

71

'Outside.'

'Where? To look at those bloody owls again? I swear you spend more time looking at those owls than at me.'

He left her. She followed him, in her slippers, barely dressed. It was dark out. He ignored her. He went to the owl pens.

In the dark he could hardly see them, only the white ones. He made his way to the pen of his favourite. If he stared and he stared he could make out the pale moon-slip of her beak.

'What are you doing?' Iris whispered.

Wesley tried to see the owl more clearly but his eyes weren't yet adapted. He could hear the others, though. Ghostly trills. Occasional squeals.

'It's worse at night, don't you think?' he asked. 'To keep them here?'

'What?'

'People watch them during the day and they don't seem too bad, but at night, that's their time. That's when they wake and want to fly.'

Iris crossed her arms over her chest. It was cold out here.

'I'm haunted,' Wesley said, eventually, 'by things that happened in the past.'

'What things?' Iris asked. 'Why won't you tell me, Wes?'

'I lost my right hand,' Wesley said.

'What?' Iris was confused now.

'People kept leaving me. When I was a boy.'

'Your dad?' she said, trying to follow him.

'And all the time,' he said, 'I wanted to try and find the thing I'd lost. Searching. Searching. Punishing everyone.'

'What?' She was shivering now. It was cold. It was cold.

'But I'll tell you,' he said, 'that I've finally realized

something. All the time I thought I was punishing others I was actually only punishing myself, but not *properly*.'

He was trying to see the owl in the darkness. He could make out her shape now.

'Let's go in,' Iris said. 'Let's talk inside.'

He turned to face her. 'I must do something,' he said, 'to show you how much I love you.'

'What?' He had lost her, completely.

'For the baby,' he said.

He stretched open his right hand in front of her face. For a moment she was frightened that he might try to hurt her. He might hit her or smother her with that hand. But then he turned from her and slowly, deliberately, finger by finger, he pushed his hand into the wire mesh of that giant and wakeful emu-owl's cage.

He could see his white fingers in the darkness, and finally, too, he could see her. She could see him. She was still. She was silent. He heard one of the other birds calling and then she was on him. Ripping and tearing with her beak like a blade.

Iris screamed.

She couldn't forgive him. On his right hand was left only a thumb. She griped that she'd almost lost their child with the shock of it. He apologized. Over the following months he kept apologizing. He stopped pouting. He couldn't stop smiling now. Sometimes she'd catch him touching his spoiled hand with his good one, talking to himself, but so softly, like it was a child's face he was stroking.

On the night their baby was born he left her. An envelope lay on the bed. Her parents found it and brought it to her. Inside was a cheque for several hundred pounds and a note which said only: 'Heading Inland'. That was all.

The Piazza Barberini

Tina was doing Rome on a budget. Her companion was horrible. He was called Ralph. She met him accidentally, and he stuck to her like a burr, like a leech, until he grew bored of her. Then he let go, just as suddenly.

He had, she discovered, over seven different ways of describing the rectum. His favourite was ring which he used and used until it was quite worn out. Ironically – she just *knew* this was funny – Ralph was actually an arsehole himself. But she was too polite to say anything. He even looked like an arsehole. Not literally, but he wore dark glasses, a furry trilby – right there, on the back of his head, monstrously precarious – and thick-soled loafers. She presumed that he thought his look was, in some way, Italian. She knew better. Even the Italians knew better.

Ralph was staying at a *pensione* south of Termini. It wasn't particularly salubrious around there. Tina didn't like it. She, by contrast, was staying in Old Rome, in the heart of Rome, close to the fruit market, the best piazza, the better cafés.

Tina had met Ralph while she was queueing for the Vatican Museum. It had been a ridiculously long queue, but she presumed that the wait would be worth it. Ralph had joined the queue behind her, had introduced himself, had asked whether she'd mind saving his place for him while he popped off for a minute, then disappeared. An hour later, when she'd nearly reached the front, he reappeared again. She'd completely forgotten about him by then. She almost didn't recognize him. His glasses were pushed up on to his head. His eyes – bold, empty – stared at her: a mucky brown. Two round hazelnuts. He said he didn't have quite enough money for the entrance fee – 'What? You're kidding! That much?' – so she paid for him on the understanding that he'd pay her back later.

He never did. Ralph was from Reading. He worked for British Telecom. He had a smattering of Italian. He could order coffee, ice-cream, several flavours of pizza, without even consulting his guidebook.

Tina felt sorry for him. He wore a Lacoste polo shirt, but it wasn't actually Lacoste because the alligator was facing the wrong way. She knew about these things. She was training to be a buyer at Fenwicks, New Bond Street, London. Ah, yes.

Ralph tried to persuade Tina to have a piece of brightly coloured cotton twine plaited into her hair on the Spanish Steps. Several men, unkempt, like hippies, were offering this service for a small sum.

'I'd rather not,' she said, noticing their dirty hands, their tie-dyed shirts. 'I think I might just climb up to the top of the steps and look at the view.'

Ralph followed her. He was like a naughty spaniel; bored, precocious, snapping at her heels.

The view was fine. When they'd had enough of it, Ralph said, 'I wanna take you somewhere special. It's called the Piazza Barberini. It's not far from here, just down the hill. When she was in Rome, Sophia Loren used to live nearby.'

He took hold of her arm. Tina allowed herself to be led. She followed him obligingly because it was a pretty street, a steep, deep incision into the hillside. Grand houses frowned out on either side of them.

She was too obliging. What kind of girl, after all, takes any trip on her own? A bold girl? A silly girl? Oh, she wanted to be both, for once. Even Ralph, even he was a step in the right direction. A step, and she was on a trip, a voyage. Rome, she knew, held something special just for her: a fresco, a figurine, a shady walkway, an orange tree. If she kept on looking, she would find it.

In the Piazza Barberini she paused for a moment to stare at a fountain.

'I've got fountains,' Ralph said, contemptuously, 'spouting out of my brush.'

Close by was a second, smaller fountain which was covered in big carved bees. 'That,' Tina said, pausing for a moment, 'is very sweet.'

'Yeah.' Ralph walked on.

'And if it was in London,' she said, 'it would be covered in bird dirt. They don't seem to have pigeons here, or if they do, they don't mess nearly as much.'

'In Rome,' Ralph said, conversationally, 'you're only considered gay if you're passive during sex. If you screw other men, but aren't screwed, then you're not gay.'

Tina scowled. 'That's disgusting.'

Ralph grinned. 'In Italy the men are men and the women are glad of it.'

Tina rolled her eyes. She decided that Ralph had been in Rome for too long. He'd been here a week already. She'd arrived a mere thirty-six hours ago. She was glad that she was staying for only five days. After seven days Ralph was bored. He seemed incapable of seeing the prettiness around him. He was growing cynical. He didn't appreciate how good the weather was.

Ralph led Tina towards a church – In Rome, she thought, what else? – and up some steps. At the top, slightly out of breath, he turned and proclaimed, quite seriously: 'Here lies dust, ashes, nothing.'

'What?'

'It's written on the wall,' he said. 'Inside. I kind of liked it.'

She moved towards the entrance. 'No,' he said, turning from her, 'not there. This way.'

Ralph cut to the right, through a small door and down into rock, into a clammy darkness.

The stairs were steep. She followed. 'The friars here,' he said, over his shoulder, most informative, 'had cappuccino named after them.'

'Why is that?'

'Bugger knows.'

It was musty and dusty. At the foot of the stairs lay a cramped, airless, stone chamber. It had been transformed, very badly, in an almost purposefully amateur way, into a shop. There was a till and a rack of cards. Nothing much else.

A friar appeared, as if by magic, silently, out of the stonework. He was draped from head to foot in mud-coloured hessian. He stood in front of Tina and blocked her way. He stood close to her, too close, invading her personal space with the kind of bald insolence and gall that only a religious man could muster. She could tell by his eyes that he spoke no English. *She was a stupid girl*. That's what his eyes said. *She didn't understand anything*. He wanted to compress her, to liquidize her. He hated her.

In his hand the friar held a bucket. In the bucket were coins. He shook the bucket. He had a grey beard. Blue eyes. Tanned skin, like leather. He came from another century. Tina kind of hated him, too, somehow.

She put her hand into her pocket and pulled out some money. 'Give him something small,' Ralph said, materializing next to her but making no effort to contribute himself. 'You have to give a donation.' She threw some coins in. The friar shook the bucket again, more vigorously this time. Tina took out a few extra lire and tossed them in. The friar grunted, still giving an impression of intense dissatisfaction, before turning his back on her.

'This way,' Ralph said, his voice rippling with enthusiasm. 'Through here.'

From the chamber, to the right, was a short passageway. This was a crypt, Tina decided, a real crypt. It smelled of soil. Of course. On the floor was a thin coating of brown earth.

'That's specially flown in,' Ralph said, kicking it up with his loafers, 'from Jerusalem.' He snickered.

Brown. Everything was brown. Everything was wooden. It felt like a Spanish villa: whitewashed walls and dark bark. All this stuff. Candles, soil, *stuff*.

'Not wood,' Ralph said, as though he could sense what she was thinking. 'Not wood. *Bone*.'

Bones. Hundreds of hip bones, delicate, like oyster mushrooms, arching in an extraordinary design, a beautiful design, across the ceiling. Ribs as lamp fitments. Vertebrae as candelabra. One wall was only skulls. Thousands of skulls balanced one on top of another on top of another.

Tina walked, numbly, dumbly, from chamber to chamber. Some contained friars, like the one outside but recently deceased, still in their hessian, hands suppliant, fingers, fingerbones. Some were newly buried, thinly covered, freshly coated in soil.

Angels hung, corpse-like, soggy, badly, ugly . . . oh dear. Their wings were collar bones. They flew under bone arches. Tina walked, from chapel to chapel, smelling earth and death and candlewax.

'Four thousand!' Ralph whispered. 'Over four thousand dead Capuchin friars in this small place!'

Tina felt full of skin. Full of moistness. Kind of fleshy and watery, but also dead inside. She was walking through Death's rib-cage. The whole world was bone and she was such a tiny part of it. In the final chamber, two arms were hung on the wall. Ready to chastise, ready to embrace. Mummified.

Where was Ralph? Behind her?

'Watch this,' he said, leaning over, putting out his hand, grasping a bone, yanking and pulling. The friar Ralph engaged with was headless, was armless, was a sagging punch-bag of dust and rot. The bone Ralph yanked at emerged from the neck of a rotting cassock, but it could've come from anywhere, originally. It was approximately eight or ten inches long – as round, skinny and hollow as a penny whistle – and when it snapped, it gave out a crunching sigh, like the sound a slightly soggy dog biscuit might make if held in eager jaws.

'Ralph! Stop it! Leave it!'

'Hey! Tina!' Ralph said, dancing in front of her and holding the bone to his lips like it was a little pipe he would play.

He puffed out his cheeks and his fingers flew up and down it.

Tina took two steps back. Her eyes were wide. She was mortified. Ralph! She didn't like him, not one bit. She hadn't trusted him all along. She'd never met anyone from Reading before. He was as foreign to her as pesto or tagliatelle or tiramisù. Just as strange and inexplicable.

Tina turned and stumbled away from him, staggered at first but then found her feet, found herself moving faster and faster, picking up speed from chapel to chapel. Wanting, needing fresh air. *Had to get out. Where was the friar? Nowhere. Was Ralph following? Didn't seem to be.*

Soil flew upwards and outwards in an arc, some of it she kicked with her heels against the back of her calves where it slid and it niggled, down her socks, into her shoes. Soil from Jerusalem. She kept on running.

It was so hot.

Tina was in her hotel room. The window was open. The nets were shifting, shuffling in the breeze.

She had pulled off her shoes and her socks. Her feet were itching. She dusted them with her hands, delved between her toes with the tips of her fingers. Her mind was still dipping and churning.

Where was Ralph? Why had he done that? Should she have intervened? Should she have stopped him? He was hateful. She imagined him, still laughing and grinning, relentless, in his own hotel, south of Termini. She wouldn't see him again.

Tina kept touching her lip, which felt, repeatedly, as if a cobweb was dangling from it, a silky strand, a tiny feather, tickling her, irritating her. She hoped she wasn't getting a cold sore.

She felt lonely. That was stupid. She touched her lip.

'I must stop doing that.' She felt heavy. 'Stop this. You're being silly.'

She clambered on to her bed, fully dressed, lay down

flat and closed her eyes. 'Thank God,' she muttered resolutely. 'Thank God I'm not a Catholic. Thank God I'm just a buyer at Fenwicks, New Bond Street, London.' She turned over and sighed.

Tina dreamed. Tina dreamed she was doing Rome on a budget. Her companion was horrible. He was called Ralph. She met him accidentally and he stuck to her like a burr, like a leech, until he grew bored of her. Then he let go, just as suddenly.

And when Ralph let go – this was the good part – Tina met Paolo. In the botanical gardens. Paolo was half-American, half-Italian, a doctor and an amateur botanist. He was dreamy.

The day after the dust, the bones, the dirt and the death of the Piazza Barberini, Tina consulted her guidebook over an espresso and then picked her way slowly and cautiously through the via della Lungara to the botanical gardens in Trastevere.

You see, Tina knew that Rome held something special, just for her – a fresco, a figurine, a shady walkway, an orange tree – and that if she searched for it she would find it.

The weather was temperate. Plants were growing. Everything looked glorious in the Italian sunshine. The trees and the specimens were extremely well labelled. Tina wandered around the botanical gardens, smiling to herself, trying to expel all thoughts of candlewax and hessian and dark bark from her mind. And Ralph. Him especially.

Inside one of the greenhouses a smart group of horticultural Italians – smelling of starch, scent and shoe leather – were inspecting the finalists in an orchid exhibition. Tina slipped in to take a look.

The orchids seemed alien, like sophisticated intergalactic

creatures. They didn't look real. Tina squatted down in front of one, closed her eyes and inhaled. The air was warm and smelled only of soil. *Soil*. She shuddered.

'You know, that orchid is a colour you see nowhere else on this earth apart from in one other place. It is a purple-brown the colour of the human kidney, *sì*?'

Tina looked up.

'I'm Paolo. Hi. I could see you were not with the others. I guessed you were English from your shoes. Am I correct in so guessing?'

'Oh.' Tina looked down at her suede moccasins and then back up at Paolo again. 'Uh . . . The flowers were so lovely . . .'

'Orchids.'

'Yes. They almost look . . . plastic.'

'I suppose you could say that. God is a master technician, huh? I should know, I'm a doctor. I studied in America for several years, in Boston.'

'Your English is excellent.'

'Thank you. I enjoy the chance to, ah, take it out for a test drive every so often.'

Paolo shrugged his strong, square shoulders. Tina smiled.

'Your hair is in such a pretty style,' Paolo said. 'The English are so original.'

Tina put a hand to her pale brown bob. Paolo's beautiful dark eyes clouded over, momentarily.

'You must think me so presumptuous. You have not even had the chance to introduce yourself.' Paolo took hold of Tina's hand. 'Your name?'

'Tina.'

'Forgive me, Tina.' He kissed her fingers, so softly that she barely felt his lips, just his breath, which later, she discovered, was sweet and nutty and flavoured with pistachios.

Was this the thing? Was this the thing Rome held just for her? Not a fountain or a figurine, but Paolo? He took her for coffee and then invited her to collect wild mushrooms with him that afternoon in the Parco Oppio. Tina floated back to her hotel clutching a moist amaretto biscuit in one hand and something that felt suspiciously like the key to Paolo's heart in the other.

The haughty Italian matron who presided over the front desk in Tina's hotel obligingly changed some of Tina's pounds into lire and then announced, in her clipped English: 'A man came for you earlier. He left no name but he was wearing something full of . . . fluff, on his head, a hat,' she grimaced, 'and shoes made of plastic. He is . . . uh . . .' Unable to find the right word, the woman twirled her finger in a circle and raised her eyes skywards.

'Mad?' Tina tried.

'*No.*'

'English?'

She shrugged. '*Sì.*'

'Did he leave a message?'

'*Sì.*' The woman offered Tina a folded piece of paper. Tina opened it up. In badly formed letters was written:

> Tina I've gotta see you It's urgent
> love ralph

Tina turned the note over, picked up a stray, yellow Bic pen from the desk and wrote:

Ralph, At last I think I've found what I was looking for in this magical city of Rome. I won't waste your time or mine by describing what it is, but I am quite certain of what it isn't. It isn't a short Englishman in stack heels with a bad haircut and dirty teeth. I know that now. What you did in that church yesterday appalled me. I've decided I don't want to see you any more. You disgust me. Goodbye.

Tina

Tina handed the notelet back to the woman. 'If he comes by again,' she said sweetly, 'will you make sure that he gets this?' Then she slipped the Bic pen, without so much as a second thought, into her jacket pocket.

Paolo pushed aside a bush and whistled to himself. 'Do you see what I see, Tina?'

Tina recoiled. There was something about this fungus, something that made her palms dampen. Paolo put out his hands and gently plucked the mushrooms. 'With strips of pasta, some garlic, hard cheese . . . a touch of single cream.' He kissed the air and then plopped the mushrooms into the basket he was holding.

'They look a little like . . . uh . . . bones,' Tina said. 'Don't you think?'

'They taste like flesh,' Paolo said, standing up and striding off. 'Very rich, very strong, very gamey.'

Tina followed a short distance behind him. She caught up at the next bush. 'This is a nice park. Are we close to the Colosseum?'

Paolo pushed aside the bush but there were no mushrooms underneath, only a used soft drinks can and the plastic segment of a syringe. He stood to attention.

'You don't want to come here at night. Homeless people haunt this place. That is why I hunt here for mushrooms, because others don't have the audacity to look in such a venue. So you have to be observant,' Paolo added. 'Especially a woman on her own. That makes you extremely vulnerable.'

He stalked off again. Tina followed. 'Actually,' she said, 'I've found Rome very hospitable. I mean . . .'

'A woman came into my surgery yesterday,' Paolo said. 'She had been mugged while walking through the Jewish Ghetto. They wanted her watch. She resisted. They sliced into her arm with a blade, through the tendons, down to the bone. The blade was rusty. I knew even then it would go septic, get infected, start to swell and rot like garbage in the stinking heat of an Italian summer.'

'My God.'

'You must be wary. To you this is simply a holiday, but to the casual vagabond and thief, you are a perfect financial opportunity.'

Tina, from the corner of her eye, noticed what she thought might be a cluster of wild mushrooms, but they were sprouting alongside something that bore a startling resemblance to a clump of dog shit and she couldn't bear the idea of drawing Paolo's attention to them, not even for the thrill of earning his approbation.

'Have you noticed what I've noticed?' Paolo stood still, like a bloodhound, his nose flaring, his fists tightening. Tina's heart sank. He'd seen the mushrooms. Before she could respond, however, Paolo whispered, quite urgently, 'As I was saying, this place is new to you and so the sights and the pleasures of the senses are here to be enjoyed for the very first time, but I . . . I am more familiar with this environment so can take in the larger view, the periphery. Someone is following us. Did you see him? When I bought you your *gelato* he stood a little distance away. Later he bought one for himself.'

Paolo pointed. Tina followed the line of his finger. She failed to detect anything unusual.

'See?' Paolo asked. 'In the scruffy clothing, with his long face, his dirty arms. He has a pronounced limp. He's ducking behind that yellow flowering bush. He knows I'm on to him. A junkie. Probably a thief.'

Tina looked again. A man with a child and a suitcase. A young woman sitting under a tree reading a magazine. Two teenagers playing with a frisbee. And then she saw him. *Ralph*!

She nearly swore, but she stopped herself. 'Paolo!' she exclaimed. 'Over there! See? Some mushrooms.'

Paolo looked where she'd indicated, strode over, crouched down and plucked them from the soil. 'Such a meal I will make you!' he exclaimed. 'Such a feast!'

By the time he'd straightened up again, Ralph had made himself scarce. Tina blinked and wondered if she'd dreamed him.

She went home to change for dinner. Ralph was loitering outside her hotel. He was holding an open copy of *La Moda* in front of him but he wasn't reading it.

'What do you want, Ralph? Didn't you get my note?'

His face was pale and moist. He seemed distracted.

'Yeah,' he said, 'and to be honest . . .'

'I don't like being followed around,' Tina said, emphatically.

'So who the hell is that guy?' Ralph interjected indignantly. 'Christ, you're a fast worker. Yesterday it was me, today it's some fat Italian with hair sprouting out from his cuffs and his collar.'

'It was never you, Ralph,' Tina said haughtily as she pushed past him and stepped into the hotel's revolving doors. Ralph was nimble though, quick on his feet, and he stuck to her, entering the same little segment of the doors. He was crushed up against the back of her as she pushed and walked. He smelled of Dettol. Then he stopped and the door jammed. Tina tried to keep moving but Ralph was too strong. The glass held fast.

'Stop pressing against me! Let me out of here.'

'Tina,' Ralph said, 'I regret what I did yesterday. And I want to give you that money I owe you from the Vatican Museum.'

'Keep it. I don't want it.'

Ralph put his hand into his pocket and drew out an old tissue, a bus ticket, a couple of lire and a cheese straw. Tina blinked and focused. It wasn't a cheese straw. It was a bone.

'My God! What is that? Did you *steal* it?'

'Uh . . . ?' Ralph looked down. 'It's a cheese straw.'

'Oh.' Tina felt claustrophobic and slightly dizzy. 'I thought it was the bone. I mean, I thought you had the bone.'

Ralph guffawed. 'That's one way of putting it.' He adjusted his position. Tina squinted at him, somewhat perplexed. Close up, she found his white skin, his dead eyes, particularly distasteful.

'My friend thought you were a drug addict,' she said, sharply. 'You look a mess.'

'Fine,' Ralph responded. 'So I'm sorry about the way things turned out yesterday. But that note you left . . . See,' he bared his teeth, 'my mouth is spotless.'

'But your shirt,' Tina smiled back, tight-lipped, jabbing

at his chest with her middle finger, 'isn't Lacoste. It's a second-rate impersonation. Which, to be brutally honest, Ralph, seems entirely appropriate.'

While Ralph paused to digest this information, Tina took her chance and gave the door a violent shove, pushed it forward and snapped out of the restrictive glass bubble into the foyer. Ralph was disorientated for a moment but then quickly followed. He didn't let up. He trailed her to the front desk.

'Go away, Ralph.'

'It's only . . .'

She spun around. 'What?!'

He was still holding the bus ticket and the cheese straw in his right hand.

'It's only, I mean . . .' he said, shiftily. 'Couldn't we talk this over in private?'

'Get lost, Ralph.'

Ralph didn't budge. Tina asked for her key and then pressed for the lift. 'By the way,' she said sharply, 'Paolo said Sophia Loren never lived in the Piazza Barberini. She never even lived in Rome. It's just a myth. My guide-book says the same thing.'

Ralph opened his mouth to say something, but before he'd uttered a single syllable, Tina had swept off, up the stairs, taking them two at a time.

The lift arrived. The doors opened. People got out. The doors closed. Ralph remained where he was. He grimaced, looked around him, cleared his throat and then gently, neatly, *carefully*, he folded up his copy of *La Moda*.

'It looks fantastic, Paolo,' Tina murmured. She was sitting in his spotless flat and staring down at a steaming plateful of pasta and mushrooms.

'Tuck in,' Paolo said, turning this little smidgen of colloquial English over on his tongue like an exquisite truffle. Tina picked up her fork. She ate a small strand of the pasta and then smiled. 'It's delicious.'

Paolo beamed at her.

She speared a mushroom. She inhaled deeply and lifted the mushroom up towards her lips. She could smell it. It didn't smell like a mushroom at all. It smelled of old bone. Rotten bone. She paused.

'What's wrong?'

Tina closed her eyes for a moment. Don't blow it, Tina, she thought frantically. This man is a dream. You've arrived, girl. You've arrived! But her brain took no account of these thoughts and projected the unpalatable image of a dog's anus on to the inside of her eyelids. Her gorge rose.

'Tina?'

She opened her eyes. 'Paolo?'

'Is something wrong? Is it the evening light? Is it too bright?'

'The light?' Tina blinked. 'Oh. Yes, it is bright.'

'Easily remedied.'

Paolo sprang up and over to the window to adjust the blinds. While he was distracted, Tina grabbed her handbag from the floor, yanked it open and tipped the mushrooms from her plate straight into it. This whole manoeuvre took a total of four or five seconds.

She snapped the bag shut.

'Tina!' Paolo expostulated. Tina squeaked and looked up guiltily. But Paolo was not staring at her. He was staring out of the window. 'Tina, come here for a moment.'

She did as he asked. Paolo pointed. 'It's him, huh? You see him?'

Tina craned her neck and followed the line of Paolo's index finger.

'You see him? The same one as earlier. Next to the street lamp. Smoking.'

Ralph. Next to the lamp-post; bad shoes, bad hair, puffing on a cigarette. Something was wrong, though. It was his hat. It wasn't on his head, perched jauntily, as one might have expected; it was hanging from his belt buckle like a furry codpiece.

'I have reason to believe that man is stalking you,' Paolo said. 'I have every reason to believe it.' Without another word he strode swiftly from the room.

'Hang on a second . . . Paolo?'

The door slammed. Tina returned to the window. After a short time, Paolo appeared in the street. Ralph gave a start, grabbed hold of his hat, turned on his heel and ran. Paolo followed, but didn't venture beyond the end of the road. Tina went back to the table, sat down and picked up her fork.

Of course he insisted on escorting her home. He told her how one of his uncles had been glassed in the Palazzo Nuovo for his cufflinks. 'People see you, Tina, and straight away they can tell you are green. You are green like a dollar sign. A big, green dollar sign walking down the road.'

He frog-marched her into the hotel foyer, watched as she picked up her keys, called the lift. While they waited for it he arranged to meet her early the following morning for breakfast. He kissed her ear as the lift doors opened. 'Don't leave the sanctuary of the building until I am here to meet you, OK?'

Tina smiled and nodded. Paolo was so *protective*. It gave her goosebumps.

'You are so desirable,' he muttered, 'so damn vulnerable. You are an accident, Tina, just waiting to happen.'

Tina had a shower, wrapped a towel around her midriff and then strolled into her bedroom.

'My God!'

Paolo was sitting, bold as brass, on the end of her bed.

Tina clutched at her towel. 'Paolo! What on earth are you doing here?'

Paolo clucked his tongue and shook his head. 'The window. You left it wide open. I was checking the rear of the building. I came up by the fire escape. You must be more cautious, Tina. I could have been anybody.' He stood up. 'I'm sorry to have to scare you like that. It's just that we can't be too careful, huh?'

Tina nodded.

Paolo returned to the window, swung his leg over the ledge and jumped out on to the escape. 'OK,' he said. 'Tomorrow. Breakfast.'

Tina nodded again.

'The window. Close it tight, sì?'

'I will. Straight away.'

She closed it. She sat down on her bed.

'Is that guy some kind of a fucking psychopath or what?'

Tina froze and then she yelled.

'Aiuto!'

In the short silence that followed an accent that was distinctly English and distinctly Ralph's said, 'And what the fuck does that mean?'

Tina squatted down. A loafer was visible, protruding from the end of the bed.

'What the hell are you doing under there?'

Ralph was silent for a moment and then he said gently, 'I think I'm dying.'

'You're what?'

'Dying. I climbed in. You were in the shower. I needed to talk to you. Then I heard someone else climbing up the escape, so I scrambled under here. Then he sat down on the bed and now I'm stuck.'

'Stuck? How?'

Ralph cleared his throat. 'To put it bluntly, I have an erection and it's stuck inside the mesh on the underside of the mattress. It's like chicken wire or something.'

'You've got a what?'

'I've got an erection.'

Tina recoiled. She grabbed hold of her clothes, her jacket, her shoes, and dashed into the bathroom. She shot the bolt and got dressed. When she'd finished dressing she called through. 'If you've not gone by the time I count to ten, Ralph, I'm going to scream and scream until the police come.'

'One.' She put her ear to the door to listen out for his response. 'Two.' She could hear him speaking but not what he said. 'Three.' She pulled the door open a fraction.

'Four.'

Ralph's loafer protruded, as before. He had not moved.

'Five.'

'What's the guy's name, anyway?' Ralph asked, apparently unruffled by Tina's little display.

'None of your business.'

'Funny name. Must be foreign.'

Tina scowled. 'Paolo.'

'Paolo?' Ralph snorted. 'He's so fucking paranoid. More to the point, he's so *hairy*. Even his ankles. I was staring at his ankles for a full five minutes while you were still in the shower and, I'm not kidding you, the hair was half an inch thick. It was extraordinary. Staring at his ankles was the only thing that stopped me from screaming myself stupid.'

Tina paused and then addressed herself emphatically to Ralph's loafer. 'Paolo has every reason to feel paranoid on my behalf. I have a strange man stalking me, pestering me, hiding under my bed while I'm in the shower . . .' Modesty forbade her to mention the erection.

'And the erection,' Ralph said. 'Don't forget about that.'

He twitched his foot. Tina stared at it malevolently. The thick sole, the scuffed heel. Slip-ons, she thought. So common. They were brothel creepers, really, with a large ornamental buckle glued on the side. Nasty, stupid shoes.

'Anyhow, Paolo's a doctor,' Tina muttered, dragging her eyes from Ralph's footwear. 'Doctors are caring by *nature*. It's an instinct.'

'A *doctor*!' Ralph parroted. 'How *gratifying* for you.'

He was quiet for a while and then he said, 'You wouldn't happen to have a pair of nail clippers handy, would you?'

'Nail clippers?'

'So I could try and cut myself free.'

Tina looked churlish but picked up her bag anyway and was about to open it but then paused. 'I don't know if I want you cutting yourself free. You might be dangerous.'

Ralph snickered. 'Let's get one thing straight between us, Tina. I had no interest at all in ever seeing you again after our little bit of fun in the crypt yesterday. And although I have an erection, that's no reason to think I find you irresistible.'

Tina tucked her bag under her arm and headed for the

93

bathroom. She'd just remembered Paolo's mushrooms and wanted to clear them out over the sink to minimize the mess.

'What are you doing?'

'Finding some clippers.'

'Oh.'

Tina grabbed some tissues and pulled the bag wide. She paused. She stared.

'Oh, shit.'

In her bag, instead of the mushrooms she'd expected, there were ten finger bones. Ten clittery-clattery finger bones. Yellow bones. Earthy bones.

She dropped the bag.

Ralph was still talking. Tina wasn't listening. She backed away from the sink, out of the bathroom, into the bedroom and gently pushed the door shut. When she next spoke her voice was low. 'I couldn't find any clippers after all.'

'Great.' Ralph sighed. 'So now what?'

Tina grimaced. 'If you leave yourself alone for a few minutes maybe it'll have a chance to go down.'

'It won't go down. It has no intention of going down. That's what I've been trying to tell you.'

Tina said nothing, only stared peevishly up at the lamp fitment. Ralph continued talking, undaunted. 'You don't know the half of it.'

'I don't want to know. I'm not interested. I just want you out of here.'

'So I got home to my hotel yesterday,' Ralph said, his voice slightly muffled by the bed and the mattress, 'sat down, dozed for a while and then *ching*! A hard-on. Well that's hardly anything out of the ordinary. So I grappled with it for a while, but the more I touched it the harder

94

it got. And it wasn't a good hard. It was a bad hard. It was angry. I couldn't relax. It hurt if I sat down, it was even worse if I stood up. It *burned*. And it wasn't a sexy feeling, just kind of irritating. Eventually I started to get depressed. Frustrated too. But then out of the blue, after a few hours struggling, I found relief. Want to know what it was that relieved me?'

Tina's lip was tingling. She curled it. 'Desperately.'

'You. It was you.'

She recoiled.

'Funny, huh? As soon as a thought of you flitted into my mind I felt a kind of *loosening*, I mean, it didn't go down or anything but the discomfort eased a bit. But it kept me up all night just the same. And I felt weak. Like all the blood had been diverted from my body and brain into just that particular part of me.'

Tina smirked but said nothing.

'In the morning I walked over to your hotel. I left you the note. In the foyer it stopped hurting altogether. Strange, huh?' He paused. 'So you don't even have some scissors handy?'

'No.'

'Well, can you try and lift the bed then? It feels like I'm being garrotted.'

Tina appraised the bed. It was large and heavy and the headboard was a thick, dark wood. She squatted down. 'There's no way I can lift this thing. It's huge. You're just going to have to untangle yourself.'

Ralph fiddled quietly for a while. The sound of his nails against the mattress wire set her teeth on edge. She stared over at the bathroom door.

'Have you ever had a 24-hour erection before, Ralph?'

Ralph stopped fiddling.

'Nope.'

'Maybe you should go to a doctor or something.'

'Why? Fancy calling Paolo over?'

Tina's thoughts turned to Paolo. She touched her bottom lip with her index finger and dwelt on his pistachio-flavoured kisses. Her fingers, she noticed, after a short interval, smelt very strongly of soil. *Soil*? She stared at her hands. They were clean. They were spotless.

'I'm only saying,' Tina continued, slightly anxious now, 'that you snapped that bone yesterday and ever since . . .'

Ralph chuckled. From under the bed his laughter sounded like a mouse scampering. 'Have you got bones on the brain or something?'

'You snapped that bone and now you have this strange *stiffness*.'

'The penis doesn't have a bone in it, Tina. It's blood that makes it hard.'

After a pause, Ralph added, 'I guess it's just one of those things. We don't much like each other but in some weird way we're destined to be together.'

Tina struggled to stop herself from growling.

'Fate,' Ralph sighed, and then tapped his foot against the mattress.

Tina felt claustrophobic. She walked to the window. 'So why do I keep seeing bones everywhere?' she asked, almost piteously. 'And why does this whole room reek of soil? Damp soil. Can't you smell it?' She yanked the window open.

Ralph sniffed obligingly. 'Smells of old cum and moth-balls under here.'

'We're cursed!' Tina exclaimed dramatically, half meaning it, half not.

'Bullshit!' Ralph sounded utterly unperturbed. 'I don't believe in that stuff.'

'But you believe it's fate that we should be together? That's so stupid. Maybe I should call down for a porter.'

Ralph continued to fiddle. 'Great idea. Try explaining this situation in pidgin Italian.'

'I'm tired.'

'Ring Paolo, then,' Ralph said brightly. 'Explain things to him.'

Tina blinked. 'Paolo? No way.'

'Why not?'

'I'll look stupid.'

'Hardly. I'm the one looking ridiculous here, not you.'

Tina said nothing. Ralph, in turn, ruminated for a while. Then he said, quite softly, almost inaudibly. 'Maybe you're right, though, maybe I shouldn't have taken that bone after all.'

Tina froze. *'What?'*

'Perhaps I shouldn't have taken it. I should have just dumped it.'

Tina's hands formed into fists. 'You *took* the bone? Is that what you're saying?'

'Not exactly.' Ralph tried to stifle a yawn but failed. 'You did.'

Tina's hands flew to her throat. It tightened.

'You nearly slipped, remember? I thought that monk fella was coming so I tossed the bone into your jacket pocket.'

Tina stared down at her jacket. She took two deep breaths, and then slowly, fearfully, she slipped her hand into her right pocket. Inside she found some tissues and a couple of English coins. Nothing else. She exhaled her relief and then steeled herself for the left pocket. She dipped in her hand . . . More tissues, an old bus ticket, and then? Something stiff and slim and potentially fibrous. Gently, gently she withdrew it. The bone. Only it wasn't a bone, it was a Bic pen. Yellow, innocuous.

'You *bastard*!'

Ralph howled. 'Sorry,' he coughed, between gasps. 'I guess that was rather *close to the bone*!' He laughed some more. Tina said nothing. Instead she went and picked up the phone.

Most of it she explained there and then. The remainder she whispered to him outside on the fire escape, away from Ralph's prying ears. Of course he was angry. But there was a slant to Paolo's anger that Tina hadn't anticipated. It wasn't the sacrilege or the invasion of her privacy or even the lie over her former intimacy with Ralph that he minded. It was the erection.

'A 24-hour erection? No way. It is not possible.'

Paolo clambered into the room, got down on to his hands and knees and stared at Ralph and his entrapped member. Ralph shielded himself with an outstretched hand. 'What is this?'

Paolo was undaunted. 'No way. I am a doctor. I have never heard of such a thing.'

Ralph grinned, sensing Paolo's pique. 'Actually, it's been more than twenty-four hours now. It's closer to thirty.'

Paolo swore in Italian and then stood up. 'OK, turn away, Tina, I don't want you seeing anything that might prove unsettling. And you . . .' He kicked Ralph's foot.

'Ow!'

'You, get ready for me to lift the bed. I'll go slowly but prepare yourself for some discomfort.'

Tina turned away. Paolo braced himself, grunted and

then lifted. Ralph cursed and rapidly made some necessary adjustments.

'Right,' he said finally, 'I'm decent. Hold it three seconds longer, Paolo, and I'll roll out from under.'

After exactly three seconds Paolo dropped the bed, unceremoniously. Ralph tried to stand up. But before he could straighten himself Paolo had darted over and shoved him, quite forcefully, in the centre of his chest. Ralph jerked and then wilted. Paolo was at least a foot taller than he was.

'Sit! Over there. In that chair.'

Paolo pointed. Ralph winced, staggered over and sat down.

'Now what?'

'So,' Paolo glared at the significant protuberance between Ralph's thighs. 'I can clearly see that there is indeed some activity in your trousers.'

Ralph looked down at himself, as if to confirm in his own mind that this was true.

'Yes.'

Ralph's penis was stretched and erect under the fabric of his jeans.

'Tina,' Paolo said softly. 'Make yourself comfortable on the bed. I myself will take the other chair.'

Tina did as Paolo had asked. Paolo pulled a chair over to a position directly opposite Ralph's, and then settled himself into it. Nobody spoke. Finally, Tina said gently, 'It's late. Hadn't Ralph better get going?'

Ralph nodded keenly, all previous thoughts of his improbable connection with Tina patently abandoned.

'No, Tina,' Paolo replied calmly. 'Now we wait.'

Tina frowned. 'But what for?'

'We wait until his magical erection goes down. Then I will kill him.'

Ralph's eyes widened. So did Tina's. Paolo just smiled and kept his eyes fixed on Ralph's thighs. Ralph squirmed.

'Ah yes!' Paolo sneered, looking and sounding quite demonic. 'Try and maintain that erection under real pressure, little man. We'll all see how long it lasts, eh, Tina?'

Tina cleared her throat. 'But maybe, Paolo . . .'

Paolo silenced her with an impressive jerk of his eyebrow. 'You called me, Tina, and I came. This is my business now. Keep out of it.' Tina retreated back on to her pillows.

Ten minutes. Twenty minutes. Thirty minutes passed. Nothing moved except for Tina's eyes which turned every so often towards the clock on her bedside table. After forty minutes Paolo was still as watchful and focused as a kestrel in a summer wheatfield. Ralph was pale and bug-eyed and sweating. But his erection remained prodigious.

Eventually Paolo stirred. 'Tina, I need to use your bathroom.' Tina nodded. Paolo stood, went to the window and fastened it, turning the security lock at its base and pocketing the key.

'The room keys?'

Tina pointed to the bedside table. Paolo picked these up on his way into the bathroom. He closed the door behind him.

In a flash Ralph turned to her and whispered frantically. 'He's a fucking maniac! He's going to kill me. He means it. Why the fuck did you have to go and phone him?'

Tina gaped. 'Me? Why did I phone him? It was your idea in the first place. How was I to know he'd react this way? Anyhow,' Tina pointed, 'the erection's still there, isn't it?'

Ralph unzipped his fly and brought out a cheese straw.

Tina stared, dumbstruck. Finally she murmured, 'What is that?'

'What does it look like? I never had an erection. It was a wind-up. I wanted to pay you back for being such a stuck-up bitch the other day. And for passing me over.'

'Passing you over? Are you mad?'

'I was going to run off once you'd phoned him, so that he'd come round and you'd look stupid. But,' he indicated the zip on his fly, 'this fucking thing *did* get caught and I *was* stuck there for a while so then I thought, why the hell not sit this out and be in on all the fun?'

The toilet flushed. Tina gestured frantically. 'Put that back in! He's coming.'

A droplet of perspiration had formed on the tip of Ralph's nose. 'I can't. It's crumbling. It's hot down there.' He waved the straw and it drooped. Tina's hand darted into her pocket and she pulled out the Bic pen.

'Take this. Quickly.'

Ralph snatched the pen and stuck it down his trousers with dispatch. Just in time. Paolo came strolling out of the bathroom. Tina was still staring anxiously in Ralph's direction and so failed to detect that Paolo was holding something in his hands. Her bag. After a cursory glance at Ralph's genitals, he sat down in his chair again and placed the bag on his lap.

'Tina, could you possibly explain something for me?'

Tina glanced over. 'Paolo?'

'Could you perhaps explain why it was that when I went to wash my hands in your sink I found your handbag in there, and it was open, and inside it was the mushroom dinner I cooked you?'

Ralph turned and appraised Tina. His mouth had fallen

slightly ajar. Tina looked down at the counterpane. She opened her lips to say something but then Ralph spoke first.

'Actually, Paolo,' he said calmly, 'she throws up everything. It's a medical condition. She's an anorexic.'

'Bulimic,' Tina corrected him, quickly.

'That too.'

Tina chewed on her lower lip. She felt so tired. She could barely call up the strength – physical, moral – to meet Paolo's gaze. 'I'm sorry, Paolo,' she said finally, peering up beseechingly. 'It was no reflection on the meal. Really it wasn't.'

Paolo continued frowning for a few seconds longer and then suddenly he smiled. Tina smiled back. Even Ralph smiled.

'Dear Tina,' he said gently, 'you must think me a beast. I had no right to look into your bag. I'm sorry.'

His face softened and, true to form, Tina's heart – like a lump of semi-congealed butter on a warm hotplate – softened with it. Everything would be all right. She felt it, suddenly. Everything would be just fine. She turned to Ralph. 'This is ridiculous, Ralph,' she said boldly, 'and it's all gone on for long enough. We should tell Paolo about the pen. I'm positive he'll understand.'

'The pen?' Paolo's eyebrows rose.

Ralph's face was rigid. 'I don't think so, Tina,' he said slowly, his eyes fixed on her most expressively.

But Tina didn't baulk. 'It's just got way out of control,' she said firmly. 'Tell him, Ralph. Get it over with.'

'Get what over?' Paolo leaned forward in his chair, his neck extending so that the muscles stretched and pumped with all the elasticity of chewing gum.

Tina took a deep breath. 'It isn't an erection, Paolo.

Ralph's got a pen down his trousers. It was all just a stupid joke. He told me while you were in the bathroom.'

Paolo got to his feet, very slowly. 'Ralph,' he said softly. 'Over the past hour I have had the opportunity to scrutinize your clothes and your footwear at some length. Your shoes are very unusual. In Italy we don't have anything quite like them. Perhaps I could take a closer look. Would you mind?'

Ralph, paradoxically, had pushed his body as far back into his chair as it would go. He took a deep breath. He shook his head. 'Of course I wouldn't mind.'

Slowly, stiffly, he lifted up his foot so that Paolo might see one of the shoes without bending down. Paolo took hold of the foot, pulled the shoe off and quietly inspected it.

As he did this, Ralph watched him fixedly, and then, for a split second, his eyes darted sideways, towards Tina. In that instant Paolo grabbed hold of Ralph's jaw, prised his mouth open and rammed the tip of the loafer into it.

Ralph flailed helplessly, his jaw stretched wide, his eyes squeezed tight. Tina sprang up and grabbed hold of Paolo's arm. 'Stop it! Leave him alone! You'll hurt him!'

As soon as she touched him, Paolo let go. He raised his palms to the ceiling. 'See? I've let go. See?'

Tina nodded.

'Are you happy now?'

She nodded again.

'Good.' Paolo smiled. Tina tried to smile but couldn't quite manage it. Ralph? Ralph didn't even try to smile. He was too busy choking. The loafer lay in his lap, bereaved of its fancy buckle.

Tina hadn't yet noticed. Ralph, gagging, threw his shoe

at her to get her attention. He tried to cough but his throat was blocked and he couldn't exhale. Tina caught the shoe. She looked down at it and then over at Ralph who was slack-jawed and drooling.

'What's wrong?'

He clutched at his throat.

Paolo glanced down too.

'I think he's choking on something. Ah!' He pointed to the shoe Tina held. 'The buckle's come off. He must have swallowed it.'

'Oh God!' Tina dropped the shoe. 'So now what?'

Paolo shrugged. 'I suppose we should call for an ambulance.'

He walked over to the phone and picked it up. Tina watched as Ralph's complexion rainbowed from red to wine to damson to ivory. Then he fell from his chair and on to the carpet.

Tina felt sick. Ralph was writhing. She was panicking. Paolo, perfectly calm, spoke on the phone for a short interval and then returned to Tina's side.

'An ambulance?'

He nodded. 'It'll be a short while.'

'But he's choking!'

'Sì.'

'Can't you do something?'

Paolo shook his head. 'I am not insured to intervene in this kind of situation. If he dies I might get sued by the family. It could ruin me.'

'If he dies?' Tina gasped. 'You're a doctor, Paolo!'

Paolo cleared his throat. 'Roughly.'

'Roughly? What do you mean, *roughly*?!'

'I'm a chiropodist.'

Tina fell to her knees, grabbed hold of Ralph's head,

stared up at Paolo and said, 'So, fine, if you *were* a doctor, what would you do?'

Paolo scratched his head. 'I suppose I would try the Heimlich Manoeuvre.'

'Yes!' Tina exclaimed. 'How does it go?'

'I have no idea. But, uh, after I'd tried that, if it didn't work, I'd make an incision at the base of the throat and push a straw into it so that he could breathe from below the blockage.'

Ralph, meanwhile, was undergoing some kind of spasm. Tina didn't know what kind of a spasm it was, only that it looked almost biblical in its monstrosity. His face was ashen, his eyes were rolling.

Tina exploded. 'I need a knife. But I haven't got one. Do you have one?'

Paolo shook his head.

'I need something pointed. *Anything* pointed.'

Ralph clutched at his groin.

Typical, Tina thought. Even in his moment of crisis . . . But then she remembered. She grabbed at his trousers, yanked down the zip, ripped out the Bic pen and held it aloft. Ralph had started to foam and to slacken.

Tina indicated towards her own throat as she looked up at Paolo. 'Is this the place? At the bottom here? Is this it?'

Paolo shrugged. 'I wouldn't know, but I don't think shoving a bone into his throat is any way to go about it. It looks dirty and it's blunt at its tip.'

Tina scowled down at the pen. It was a pen. It was a pen. It was. She started shaking. She looked into Ralph's face. Oh God, she thought, Rome *was* holding something special just for me. Not a statue, not an orange tree, not even a shady walkway, but Ralph. Ralph!

She stared at him, fixedly. How did she feel? She *hated*

him. Ralph opened his eyes. They were the colour of two brown hazelnuts. That did it. Tina shoved his head between her knees, raised the sharp point of the Bic pen skywards, paused for one second, one long second, and then brought it down, forcefully, with as much accuracy as she could muster, into the base of Ralph's throat. It entered so easily. Ralph arched and stiffened, but she kept her hand steady.

'Stay still. Hold on.'

Tina yanked the pen out again, ripped the biro section from its centre and then firmly thrust the hollow pen shell back into the wound.

Glub.

Ralph lay still, corpse-like, flaccid. Two seconds, three seconds, four seconds, five . . . And then his chest started to rise. It rose, it rose, it rose. Air whistled through the pen's shell. In, in, in and then out.

Paolo threw himself into a chair. 'You could've killed him.'

'But I didn't,' Tina said, almost regretfully, and as she spoke she cleared a piece of clotted blood away from the pen tip. The air whistled in and it whistled out.

'Do you hear that, Ralph?' Tina whispered, conspiratorially. 'The pen's making a noise like a penny whistle. Do you hear it?' Ralph's eyes had been shut since the pen had entered him. But now, slowly, gradually, he opened them. His mouth moved, it started to form a word. Tina stared at his lips. What was he saying? Was it 'Thank you'? Was it 'Sorry'? What was it? And then she realized. Chiropodist, he said. Chiropodist! Ha. Ha. Ha.

Tina felt lead in her belly. And rage. 'Take that back, Ralph. I mean it.'

Ralph's lips were smiling. Ha. Ha. Ha.

His head remained clamped between her knees. Tina took her index finger and waved it calmly in front of Ralph's eyes. 'See this?'

He blinked yes. She took the finger and placed it over the tip of the pen shell. The shell stopped whistling. Ralph's eyes bulged. His chest stopped moving. He stopped smiling, finally.

'Want to take it back yet, Ralph?'

Ralph struggled to nod. Tina tightened her knees around his skull.

'Mean it, Ralph?'

Again, he struggled. His hands flailed, helplessly. His brown eyes, not blank, not empty any more, but saying something, emphatically. He was sincere. Just this once. He'd taken it back. He'd meant it.

Tina smiled, nodded, and casually asked Paolo how long he thought the ambulance would be.

'About four metres,' Paolo said, grinning, trying to win back her favour.

'Did you hear that, Ralph?' Tina asked softly. 'Paolo made a joke. He made a joke. Ha. Ha. *Ha*.'

Ralph wasn't smiling.

'I can hear the sirens,' Paolo said. 'Can't you?'

Tina listened carefully and then nodded slowly. 'Yes, I think I do hear them.'

The sirens grew louder. Her eyes filled with tears. They sounded strange and strong and quite beautiful. Tina sniffed, blinked, looked down for a moment, and then, so *regretfully*, and with the sweetest, the softest, the gentlest of sighs, she lifted up her finger again.

Popping Corn

'Oh!' she said. 'If I had her breasts I'd become a topless model or a cocktail waitress, or I'd go to Saint-Tropez and lie on the beach all day.'

'And get cancer.'

Mandy was sitting on the bus with her mother. They had met up outside the gym. Her mother finished work fifteen minutes before the end of Mandy's aerobics class. She waited outside by the bus stop, frustratedly watching the buses go by. Sometimes she waited for twenty minutes, occasionally longer. The gym was in Deptford.

'Breasts are for milk,' her mother said. 'You get pregnant, they fill up, you squirt it out. Like a cow.'

I wonder if it's erotic, Mandy thought, feeding babies.

Her mother added, 'When I had you my nipples cracked. They were chapped and they bled. Every time you sucked on them it felt like I'd shut them in a suitcase.'

Mandy imagined this. Breasts bare, suitcase open, packing for holiday, breasts jut forward, suitcase accidentally slams shut. Whap! Chop! Nipples sliced neatly off. Inside the dark suitcase; two soft, pink jellytots.

Then she remembered Imogen's breasts. She had seen them in the showers, and then after, when Imogen patted them dry on a pale blue towel, 36C. Small tan nipples. No unsightly blemishes or stretch marks. *She didn't wear a bra! No! Not even in the class*! Only a tight, high-cut leotard like the one Jamie Lee Curtis wore in *Perfect*.

By rights they should be down by her knees, Mandy thought, and secretly, in the back of her mind, *I wish they were!*

But the truth of it was this: Imogen could easily have no inkling of how fantastic her breasts were. She probably wished they were smaller, or that her nipples were a different shade.

I hope she thinks that, Mandy thought, imagining how it would be to carry two breasts like those around – light, soft trophies.

Mandy's own breasts were much too heavy and much too round. She wore a bra to exercise in, a terrible contraption like the kind of restraining garment people were strapped up in at mental hospitals. To stop them from hurting themselves. Surgical.

Mandy pictured herself wearing no bra for the class, her breasts bouncing so much that after half an hour the skin holding them to her ribs becomes slack, thin, sticky, eventually tears. The breasts break free and travel downwards in her leotard, eventually settling either side on top of her hip bones, like two fistfuls of cellulite.

Her mother said suddenly, 'When you were a kid, three or four, we were sitting on a bus, on the top deck, close to the front, and a brassy woman came up the stairs and sat close by. She had on a tight skirt, heels, blonde curls piled up high and a low-cut top, with her breasts on display, shoved together, like plums, shoved up. You stared at them for a while, all solemn, and then you turned to me and said, very loudly, "Mummy, why has that lady got a front bottom?"'

Mandy laughed. She had heard this story before, many times. Another breast story. Ha Ha. Funny breasts, tits, boobs, dugs, knockers.

One good thing about my breasts, she thought – focusing on herself again, on the two soft pieces of fat in flesh under her sweatshirt – when I drop off food from my fork, it lands on my chest instead of on my lap. Why was this so good? She couldn't decide, only knew that it was. Her breasts were a buffer zone, they protected her, padded her, covered her heart. If she ate popcorn at the cinema, eating in a scruffy way, fistfuls shoved in at once, to avoid embarrassment, she had to take care to remember to collect and consume the formal white line of fluffy kernels before lights up.

Water Marks

'You think just because you're getting married you can say that word in this house? You think that?'

Susan had repeatedly pronounced the synonym for 'copulate', loudly, unashamedly, with emphasis, and Margaret, her mother, wasn't pleased.

'For heaven's sake, Mum!'

'Fine. That's it.' Margaret picked up Susan's breakfast tray and took several steps towards the door. 'If you want to speak like that in this house then you can go and eat your breakfast in the garden.'

'Mum!' Susan started to wheedle. 'It's my wedding day. I can't eat in the garden on my wedding day.'

A sheen of perspiration had appeared through Margaret's make-up. She hadn't yet had time to apply powder. *That's* how hectic it had been all morning.

Susan added, 'Anyway, I'm not stepping outside with my hair like this. Call Leanne.'

Margaret held on to the breakfast tray, eyeing the half-finished glass of Buck's Fizz, and then swallowed down her irritation. It is her wedding day, she thought. Let her get away with it. She dumped the tray down on to Susan's bed and went to call her second daughter.

Leanne was downstairs giving Dad his pep-talk. Scott, her son, was playing on the stairs, bumping noisily up and down, one step at a time, on his skinny, bony rump. He came when Margaret called. He popped his head into Susan's room, took stock of the situation and said, 'Why does Aunty Susan's hair look so funny?'

Susan slammed her hair brush down on to her dressing-table. 'Mum, get that little sod out of here before I wring his neck.'

Margaret placed a firm hand on to the top of Scott's head. Her fingers could almost grasp his crown in its entirety. His head felt cool, like an ostrich's egg. She applied pressure, twisted him around, his head first, his body following like a small spinning top. After she had turned him 180 degrees, she pushed him gently with her knee out of the room.

'Go,' she muttered. 'Go find Grandad. Ask him if the cars are sorted.'

'OK.' He didn't seem particularly bothered.

Leanne passed him on the stairs. 'Watch out,' he said, 'Aunty Susan's got a cob on.'

Leanne stopped. 'A cob,' she said, 'is a kind of loaf, a round loaf, sort of twirly. Or it's a male swan. That's a cob.'

Scott continued his descent. 'Grandad said Nan had a cob on this morning when the champagne cork went through the kitchen window.'

'Fair enough.' She turned and climbed up, making her way into Susan's room.

Margaret was standing in the doorway, her hands on her hips. Leanne squeezed past her.

'Now what?'

'Guess.'

Susan turned to face her.

'Susan, I'm sorry, but that's exactly what you asked for.'

'What?'

'You wanted it Elizabethan.'

'I wanted Elizabethan, but I didn't want it looking like I'd shaved three inches off the hairline. It looks like I'm going bald. The top's like a bloody . . .'

'It's a bouffant,' Margaret interjected. 'That's what you'd call it.'

Leanne added, 'It's like Glenda Jackson in that film about Elizabeth I.'

'Bloody great. She looked like an old sow in that film. I hated that film.'

Margaret sighed. 'I quite liked it.'

'You would.'

Susan put up a savage hand to her hair, but only patted it. Leanne said, 'Maybe it'll look better when the veil's on.'

'Piss it.'

Margaret picked up the tray again. 'Are you going to eat any more of this?'

'No. I've got indigestion.'

Susan turned and stared into the mirror. She didn't, she decided, look anything like *herself*. Maybe that had been the idea in the first place, to look *unlike* herself. My face, she thought, looks like a bee sting. Red and puffy.

A beautician had called around first thing to do her hair, her skin, her make-up. Even her nails. She inspected her hands. The nails, at least, looked pretty and polished. She said, 'My face is still all red.'

Leanne had been pilfering the breakfast tray. She was holding a large, brown sausage between her finger and thumb, readying herself to take a bite. Susan's comment distracted her. The sausage wasn't yet quite cold.

'A facial,' she said, 'wasn't a very good idea. I mean, you should've had it two or three days ago. A facial brings

113

out all the impurities. As soon as I have one I always get loads of spots.'

'I was spotty before.'

'You look fine.' Margaret managed to sound convinced of this, adding with equal certainty, 'This is your day.'

'You should've got married in hot-pants, like me.' Leanne grinned, remembering.

'Yeah, well, I wanted to be a traditional bride. I wanted a traditional wedding. Now my face looks like a cow's arse, I don't suppose that's going to happen.'

Margaret said, 'You'll be wearing a veil. You'll look fine.'

'Where's the dress?'

Leanne was eating the sausage. It was pink at its centre. Downstairs she could hear Scott slamming the glass-panelled door between the living room and the kitchen. He's going outside, I bet, she thought. He'll mess up his suit. She said, 'I told Scott about holding your train again this morning. He promised to try and be more careful with it.'

Susan scowled. 'The little sod'll probably sit on it and have me dragging him down the bloody aisle. Where's the dress?'

'On my bed. It only arrived an hour ago. I'll go and get it.'

Margaret took the tray downstairs, knocked on the kitchen window at Scott, who was poking around in the pond with a twig, then returned upstairs to her bedroom to fetch the dress. She had laid it out on the bed earlier. It was covered in plastic but glossy inside; a pale creature in its transparent chrysalis. She picked it up carefully and took it through.

Leanne was fiddling with Susan's hair. She was saying,

'If you just leave the back down then it'll look like it always does.'

'Well, do a French plait or something, then.'

Margaret interjected, 'Simon doesn't like it when you do it that way.'

Leanne smiled. 'Last time I did it for you he said it looked like you had a randy armadillo clinging to your scalp.'

Margaret tutted. Her tongue stuck to the roof of her mouth. That's strange, she thought, I must be nervous. She lay the dress across Susan's bed and then checked her watch. 'Fifteen minutes before the car comes. I've not even powdered yet.' She put her hand up to the front of her fringe to check that she'd taken her curler out.

Leanne said, 'Don't worry, I'm doing a pleat.'

Susan grimaced at her reflection. 'Make sure it doesn't stick out. I hate it when they stick out. Makes you look like one side of your head is bigger than the other.'

Inside Susan, waging a battle with her irritability, was a little voice saying: It's going to be fine. It's going to be all right. She said, 'Leanne, switch the radio on. They always do dedications and a song for people getting married on Radio One at this time on a Saturday. Gary Davies or someone.'

'Let me pin this in first.'

'I'll miss it.'

She yelled, 'Mum! Can you come back in here? Can you come and switch the radio on?'

Scott wandered in. 'You want the radio on?'

Susan nodded. Leanne almost dropped the pieces of hair she was holding. Scott sat on Susan's bed and fiddled with the small radio on her bedside table.

'Just switch it on. Don't mess with the tuning.'

He switched it on. A voice said '. . . *especially Mandy and John in St Albans from the gang down at the rowing club. This is for all of you.*' The dedication was followed by the opening few strains of 'Endless Love'.

'I don't believe it. I bloody missed it. I waited twenty-four years for this moment and I missed it.'

Leanne pushed the final hairclip into the pleat and then stood back. 'Rubbish. You hardly ever listen to the radio any more.'

Susan kicked at the leg on her dressing table. 'I bet there was a request for me and I missed it.'

'I don't think anyone sent a request in. Simon didn't mention it either.'

'Maybe everyone in the office or down the pub . . .'

Leanne laughed. 'You never even mentioned it before now.'

Scott switched the radio off. Very tactful for an eight year old, Leanne thought. He then said, 'Only gits listen to Radio One.'

'Go and look up "git" in the dictionary.'

'I did earlier. It means . . .' He considered the word he was about to use. 'A comptemptible person.'

'Contemptible.' She thought about this for a minute. 'I bet it means more than that.'

Leanne was doing an evening course in Old English. She was reading 'The Nun's Tale'. Lately she'd become fascinated by the origins of words. She was considering a course in linguistics, but wasn't absolutely sure whether linguistics had anything to do with the history of language.

'Give me the bloody dress.' Susan raised her voice so that Leanne should realize that this was *her wedding day*. As a bride she had authority.

Leanne picked up the dress. Susan watched her. She took hold of the dress, bending over to grasp it, holding it in her arms like a dancing partner. When Susan snatched the dress from her, it was like she was stealing Leanne's partner in a Ladies, Excuse-me. She yanked the plastic off.

Leanne joined Scott who was standing next to Susan's small bookcase looking for a dictionary. She said, 'You must've had a dictionary for school, Susan.' Then she saw one and pulled it out. 'Git,' she said. 'Look it up again.'

Scott was grouchy but did as he was told.

'G-I-T,' she said.

Susan was surrounded by a broken blancmange of cream taffeta. She was fiddling with the seed pearl buttons.

'A hundred sodding seed pearl buttons,' she said furiously. 'Traditional my arse.'

Leanne said, 'Do you want a hand with those?' As she said this she noticed a strange stain, like a water mark, on the back of the dress. 'Scott?' She spoke casually.

He said, 'I haven't found it yet.'

'Why don't you go downstairs and let Grandad help you look? Aunty Susan's got to get dressed now.'

Scott sighed, exasperated, but closed the book and left the room. Susan was still grappling with the buttons.

Leanne inspected the stain more closely. It was seven or eight inches in diameter. It did look like a water stain. This was bad news, because water, as a consequence, probably couldn't be used to remove it. If I tell Susan, she thought, she'll go mad. But if I don't tell her . . .

'What the hell is that?'

Too late. Susan had seen it.

'I think it's a water stain or something.'

'Call Mum.'

Susan dropped the dress and sat down on the bed, thoroughly disgusted.

Leanne was accustomed to the rapidity with which Susan responded to things. For Susan, everything happened immediately – it *had* to – or not at all. If she had been a flower – her dad regularly said this – she'd be a passion flower. She'd bloom for a single day and then die. Passion flowers are beautiful, Leanne thought, but when it comes down to it, I'd rather be a lilac. The little flowers start off a dark, rich purple, fade into a lovely mauve, then turn into a bright white. Three flowers in one.

Leanne called Margaret. Margaret came in after several seconds, only half-way into her suit. She wore the skirt, a searing shrimp pink, on the knee, a nice length, good fabric.

'What?'

'The dress.'

Susan pointed. Leanne had picked the dress up. She indicated towards the water mark.

'I don't believe it. It must've been like that when they sent it.'

'I'm going to sue them.'

'You only tried it on two days ago. I didn't notice a stain then.'

'Phone them and tell them I'm going to sue.'

Leanne said, 'Is there any way of getting out a stain like this?' Margaret didn't really have a clue. She didn't know much about stains on the whole. What sort of a mother does that make me? she thought. Susan was glaring at her as though it was all her fault. She was the oldest. The oldest person was always responsible. Susan said quietly, 'I'm not going. Ring Simon. Tell him it's off.'

Leanne stared at Susan. Her nose and chin were red and her eyes were doleful. This is like a game of Mouse-Trap, she decided. Scott had the game at home; a brightly coloured plastic contraption with a large silver ball. She couldn't remember how you played it, what the rules were, but she did know for certain that once the silver ball had started to roll, the course of events was pretty much determined. She said, 'You can hardly notice it, really. There's so much material. Once your veil's on it'll stretch down way below . . .'

'Phone them and tell them I'm going to sue.'

Margaret said, 'You could probably pin a couple of folds together if the veil didn't cover it.'

Leanne watched Susan's face. This could go either way, she thought. Anger or self-pity. She hoped it would be the latter. The corners of Susan's mouth began to turn down. Her chin trembled.

'It's a botch-up. It ruins everything.'

Secretly, Susan was almost pleased. The hair, the radio . . . these things hadn't been a sufficient cause for dejection, but the dress . . . well!

Margaret stopped herself from uttering platitudes. She wanted to say, 'It doesn't matter', but, of course, it did matter.

Leanne said, 'Simon asked you to marry him that day you vomited in his car after Alton Towers. Remember? It won't make any difference to him.'

Scott rushed in. He was now wearing a button-hole. Margaret said brightly, 'The flowers have arrived. That's something.'

Scott shouted over the top of her words, 'Git. A bastard. In the sense, to beget. Hence, a bastard, fool.'

Damn, Leanne thought, that wasn't very successful.

Susan matched his yells with her own. 'Scott, bugger off!' Every time I get some attention, she thought, that little brat ruins it.

Scott stuck out his bottom lip, looked from Susan, to his mother and then back again. Margaret snatched hold of his hand and led him out of the room. She's my daughter, she thought. It's her wedding day.

Leanne said, 'Susan, just because you're the bride, doesn't mean you can get away with being rude to everybody.'

'Well, what the hell does it mean then?'

Leanne scowled. 'It means that you can get away with throwing a tantrum, but that if you're a decent person you'll decide to behave well, even though you know that you don't absolutely have to.'

Susan said, 'Leanne, you're full of shit.'

Leanne held up the dress. 'Put this on.'

'No.'

'Don't be stupid.'

'It's ruined.'

'It won't even notice once the veil's on.'

Leanne watched Susan's face. *Will she, won't she, will she, won't she?*

Susan stood up and held out her arms. Leanne helped her pull the dress on. Dad shouted upstairs, 'Nearly time now. The flowers are ready. The cars are here.'

Susan twirled in front of the mirror. The dress looked fine . . . But the stain? Once the veil was on . . . The veil was long. For a moment she understood exactly what Leanne had meant about the bride choosing to be nice. That, too, was a kind of power.

Margaret came in, fully dressed now. 'See?' she said. 'I told you it'd look just lovely.'

Susan saw herself as a scale. In her mind things were

delicately balanced. She was outside herself, looking on. Things are very carefully balanced, she decided. A small weight of irritation, frustration, fury, was outweighed, only just, by a supreme equanimity. This is as it should be, she thought. I'm a bride. I'm going to church. This whole day is about . . . love.

Margaret handed Susan her bouquet. Next she picked up the veil and helped Leanne to pin it on to Susan's head. They adjusted its pale folds. This is that special moment, Margaret thought, where a mother gets all emotional.

Susan burped, then put her hand over her mouth and said, 'I could do with a Rennie or something. My gut's all acid.'

Leanne said, 'I'll get you one after I've found my shoes and my bag. I won't be long.'

Scott was sitting on the bottom stair looking petulant. Leanne said, 'Don't get any fluff on your suit.'

He said, 'I don't like Aunty Susan.'

'She's uptight, that's all. She didn't mean to be rude.'

'What did she mean, then?'

'It's complicated.'

Scott wasn't satisfied with her answer. He said, 'So sometimes it's all right to be rude?'

'Sometimes, but only if you've got a good enough reason. We'll talk about this later, OK?'

Leanne looked around for her bag and located it on the hall table. Her shoes were neatly placed on the front doormat. She slipped her feet into them and then made her way through to the kitchen, past Dad, the flowers, the chauffeur, who was having a cup of tea. She found some indigestion tablets. Scott was trailing around behind her. She said, 'It's nearly time to go.'

'Is Aunty Susan allowed to be rude because it's her wedding day?'

'No. Yes. She's only rude because she's upset. That's all.'

She swept past him and up the stairs. Scott watched her. In his mind he was working out a simple equation. It went: Wedding=Upset=Nasty=Fine. He smiled to himself. Right.

Susan processed down the stairs. Leanne and Margaret darted around behind her like a couple of frantic swifts. Susan felt almost too grand for this house, like a misplaced princess. Her mind had been quietened by meditating solely on the letter I. I'm looking forward now, she thought. I am the present. I am the future.

The chauffeur led the way to the main car. A Rolls. White. Margaret followed, then Leanne, next to Susan, who had agreed, just this once, to hold up her own train. Grandad locked the front door.

Scott stood in the path behind Susan as they waited to arrange her comfortably in the car.

'Aunty Susan,' he said, his small voice chiming out as clearly and purely as a perfect crystal bell.

'What?' She barely turned.

He said, 'Aunty Susan, it looks like you've wee-weed all down the back of your dress.'

Susan's good intentions flew out of her mouth like a big, fat, red, angry robin.

Back to Front

Nick was back to front, but only on the inside. When he was born, the midwife held him up by his tubby, bloody legs, cleared out his mouth and his nasal passages while the doctor, holding his stethoscope, aimed it like it was a dart and Nick's heart the bulls-eye, listened, blinking, holding his own breath, for the infant's heartbeat.

But he heard nothing. Just the faintest scuddering; a faraway, dreamy sound, something so distant from the white, harsh delivery chamber, the long, tiled hospital corridors, the clatter of trolleys, the banging of doors; something so soft and fragile, so remote, that it sounded like the peripheral scuffle and bicker of two wagtails arguing over a berry in a holly bush.

He tried not to panic. Nick's mother, propped up on four pillows, whipped and battered, noticed in an instant.

'What's wrong?'

'Nothing's wrong.'

'Tell me!'

'If you'll just quieten down for a moment . . .'

The young doctor held his breath until his eyes began to water. Still that rattling noise, and very indistinct. But the child was as fresh and ripe as a little cherry, a boy, breathing and gurgling and thinking about squealing.

'I'm just going to take him off with me for a minute,'

the doctor muttered, grabbing Nick's legs and righting him. The midwife caught the doctor's eye. Nick's mother caught the midwife catching the doctor's eye. As Nick was carried from the delivery room, she struggled to count the number of his fingers and the number of his toes. Ten of each. Before he was gone.

And so it was. Nick was set apart. He was different. Outwardly, not a sign, but inside, everything back to front.

'Everything,' the doctor told the midwife, five minutes later, full of wonder, 'the opposite way around from how it should be. I couldn't hear his heart at first but it's beating well enough, except it's on the right-hand side of his body instead of on the left. And all his other organs too. Topsy-turvy. There's a name for it.' But he didn't know the name because Nick was his first.

Nick's mother, Grace, told all the other mothers how her Nick was back to front. 'I called him Nick,' she said, 'because he came along in just the Nick of time.'

The other mothers cackled. Although, in truth, there was nothing medically dangerous about Nick's condition, and time, or the lack of it, was of no consequence whatsoever.

Nevertheless, every day she counted his fingers and his toes just to make sure. Ten. Ten. She was a pernickety mother. As Nick grew older, if he complained about her coddling she'd tell him how he was taken from her on the day he was born, set aside, examined, and all the while she hadn't known what was wrong, had only imagined. And there's nothing worse than imagining. Not a thing.

So Nick was set aside and he was special, but only on the inside, and that kind of difference, the invisible kind, can be very hard to live with.

At school, his teachers found him to be a small, sharp

peak; slippery and unassailable. He was so convinced of his own superiority. And the other children had no interest in anatomy, or where exactly the heart was located. It would be a long time until that particular juncture – third form biology, maybe, but certainly not yet.

It was hard for Nick to understand his own apparent insignificance. At first he'd emphasized his difference and this had made the other children hate him. So he wouldn't fit. Didn't want to either. And then they teased, insulted and derided him. So then he couldn't fit, even if he'd cared to. But finally they began to ignore him. He became a blank. A nil. A nothing.

When Nick was aged fifteen, Grace remarried. His stepfather, Thomas Siswele, was Nigerian by birth. Grace thought Thomas was different, not ordinary like she and Nick were but, oh so special. He taught Grace how to cook groundnut stew with plantain.

And so it started. Each day Thomas would bring home the local paper and read out titbits to Grace as she prepared their dinner. He'd read out news about fêtes and fairs and infestations, an award-winning garden on the eighth storey of a tower-block, a fight, a rape, arson, theft.

You'd almost believe, Nick thought, standing in the doorway, unheeded, that he'd gone and written that paper himself, with all the fuss she makes over it.

One Friday afternoon, Nick turned himself in at the police station for shoplifting.

'What did you steal?' they asked. He told them.

'Where did you put the stolen goods?'

'In my bedroom.'

They searched Nick's house and found nothing. So he had to tell them how he'd stolen a car.

'What's the registration? The car type? The colour?'

He told them, details he'd seen in the paper. But then they found the missing car in a lock-up in Walthamstow and covered in someone else's prints.

Nick told them how he'd set fire to a factory in High Barnet. 'Why? What fuel did you use? Whereabouts and how much?'

'Petrol. Everywhere.'

But the specialists told the police that the fire had started because of an electrical fault. There were no traces of petrol.

After a while the police got sick of Nick. His time-wasting. Nick was excited by this. He kept on wasting their time hoping it would lead somewhere, but instead of charging him for it they decided to ignore him. They told him he was the boy who cried wolf. And you know what happened to the boy who cried wolf, they said, don't you? Nick prayed it would happen.

Back to front, back to front, back to front. Had to mean something.

Then he met Lyndon, in a police cell.

'What you up for?' Lyndon asked.

Nick struggled to remember. 'Armed robbery,' he said. 'Jewellers.'

'H. Samuel's?'

'That's the one.'

'Did you do it?' Lyndon already knew the answer. His question was merely a matter of form.

'Yes, I did it,' Nick said.

Lyndon eyeballed Nick while rubbing his chin. You see, this was *his* crime Nick was appropriating.

'You didn't do that job,' Lyndon said eventually. 'I did that job.'

Nick merely shrugged.

'I did that job,' Lyndon reasserted. And this was the act he'd been denying and recanting, in his own mind, to the coppers, for hours now, for days now.

'What you in for?' Lyndon asked again.

'Robbery,' Nick said, 'H. Samuel's.'

'Fuck you, man. I did that thing.'

Nick shrugged.

'Don't fuck with me, man. I did that thing.'

Lyndon was no great respecter of lies, except of his own. He squared up to Nick. Nick sighed and turned to the wall.

'What you in for, man?'

Nick said nothing. His mind was miles away, thinking about the distinction between *being* different and *doing* different. He didn't have to be, only to do.

Lyndon had no interest in distinctions of any kind. He had a small knife secreted in the sole of his trainer. He drew it out.

'What you in for?'

Nick was busy deciding in his own mind whether a plantain and a banana were the selfsame thing.

Lyndon calculated that if he stuck his knife in, just so, in that place where nothing particularly important was stationed . . . He knew the distinction, it must be admitted, between grievous bodily harm and murder. Nick had his back to him. Lyndon's knife was so sharp it slid in with ease.

Nick had arrived, finally. This was his moment. He was so happy because everyone was shouting and looking and touching and pushing and staring. Finally the crowds cleared and a doctor stood before him.

'Let's see,' he said, swabbing Nick's wound with cotton wool, assessing its relative anatomical insignificance. This was Casualty. He was busy.

Even so, Nick was losing an unusually large amount of blood. The doctor felt Nick's pulse. It was weak. He used his stethoscope. He could hear almost nothing. The faintest of sounds.

Nick stared up at the doctor, full of joy, and debated whether to tell him his secret. He opened his mouth, he breathed in, he was just about to, and then something wonderful occurred to him. Wouldn't it be great, wouldn't it be just the best thing ever, if he left the doctor to find out for himself? How exciting that would be. What a revelation!

After Nick died, the doctor spent a long while marvelling over his peculiar insides. And the coroner did, too. And the student working alongside the coroner. He'd never seen anything quite like Nick before. All back to front! Nick was his first. Nick was very special. Yes, he was. He was.

Limpets

Davy swore to himself, that day on the New Plaistow Road, that even if he lived to be one hundred years old, he would never ask a woman out again. Not like that. Not *cold*. 'Next time,' he decided, 'I'll be in a disco. I'll ask her to dance, I'll offer to buy her a drink . . .' A series of small questions. She could turn any single one of them down and he wouldn't be irreparably injured. No matter how fine she was, how pretty.

Inside the café on the New Plaistow Road, Jodi, the girl he had asked, was wiping down a table. There was only one other person in the café. He was a short, squat man, a heavy drinker. His name was Leonard.

'You bitch!' Leonard said. 'You turned him down flat, just like that. Do you know how much pluck it takes for a man to ask out a girl?'

Jodi had her back to him as he spoke. 'Are you married, Leonard?'

She knew that he wasn't. He wore a gold ring, like a wedding ring, very plain, but he was not married. Never had been. Brown and bitter was his poison. His father was Greek, his mother Italian. Both dead now. He was sixty-two years old, unemployed.

'I am not married.'

She turned and faced him, one hand held aloft,

clutching a moist cloth tightly so that no crumbs should fall from it, her other hand, open below, ready to catch.

'Can you play chess, Leonard?'

He rubbed his nose, which was puce and bulbous. She thought his nose looked as if it was riddled with wood-worm. Pores both full and black or gaping.

'No chess. Dominoes.'

'Well,' she said, having established her position in her own mind very comfortably with these two questions, having justified herself quite adequately, 'butt out.'

Davy opened his packet of cigarettes, removed one and stuck it between his lips. He squinted down at it as he fumbled in his pocket for his lighter. In his head her voice reverberated. She said, 'D'you want a can of anything to take with you?' She always said this to him when she totalled up his lunch on the till.

'Not today,' he said, breaking with tradition. 'Actually . . .'

'OK.' She was about to tell him how much he owed her.

'Actually I wanted to ask you something.'

She looked up.

'Yes?'

It occurred to Davy, at this moment, that most people would have said *what*, but she had said *yes*. Why is that? he thought. What does it mean? And then: Ask her, you fool.

'I wondered if you'd come out with me some time. I mean tonight, maybe. Or Saturday.'

Jodi put her head to one side and stared at him. Her hair was carefully arranged in the strangest style. The first time he had gone to the café he had been confused by it, suspicious. Since then, however, quite spontaneously, he had decided that he liked it. Her hair was thick, straight, black, parted viciously, pulled into two fat plaits and these plaits curled into little, neat bundles on either side of her head; thick, black limpets. It was a weird, wretched, ridiculous, Germanic hairdo.

He was fashionable himself, did his hair in a self-conscious quiff at the front, at the back, a duck's-arse. Fashionable he could understand, but strange? Had her hair been loose and straight, he would have propositioned her two weeks earlier.

Of course, Jodi hadn't even noticed him. He was only another bloody customer.

Eventually she said, 'I honestly don't think it's worth it.'

'What?'

'Put it this way . . .' She paused. He waited for her to tell him that she had a husband (no ring), a boyfriend, a sick mother. He wanted to say, 'I work as a runner for a film company up West. I'm twenty-two. I'm actually very interesting . . .'

'Imagine,' she said coldly, 'if people were like . . . if their faces were like television screens, and when any one person looked at another person they could see everything they were thinking and everything they had ever thought or said about each other. Well, if that were the case, you'd be looking at my screen, and let me tell you, right off, my screen would be completely blank. Just empty.'

Davy was silent for a moment and then he said, 'How much do I owe you?'

'Two fifty.'

He handed her the money.

'Thanks.'

She opened the till and put it inside, then picked up a damp cloth which she kept behind the counter to wipe down the tables.

He said, 'A simple yes or no would've been perfectly adequate.'

Jodi ignored this, ducked under the counter, walked to the table that he'd used and began to wipe it down.

She was too thin, he decided, and those stupid black plaits on either side of her head looked like Mickey Mouse ears.

'See you.'

He walked out, relieved that only one other person had been present in the café to witness his humiliation. An old geezer who was always there, sitting at the corner table, smoking, half-pissed. Sweaty.

It was good and cool outside. He stopped next to the edge of the kerb and scrabbled around in the pockets of his jeans for his cigarettes. Screw her! he thought. Never-a-bloody-gain. No way.

'You bitch!' Leonard said.

Jodi listened to Leonard's comments and responded appropriately. She then returned to the till, picked up a copy of *The Times*, turned it to the correct page and then folded it down to a manageable size before lounging against the counter and studying it.

Leonard stood up. She didn't raise her eyes from the paper. He was an old bastard but a regular. She trusted him.

He staggered to the door, pulled it open and then stepped outside.

'Hey. You, boy. You still hanging around here? Still after something?' He coughed quietly, drew a glob of phlegm from his throat, into his mouth and then swallowed it down. Davy was inhaling on his cigarette. He turned and looked over his shoulder at Leonard.

'Who, me?'

Leonard moved towards him. 'Tell me something,' he said. 'How come women are so fucking stupid?' He tapped the side of his head with a plump, yellowy forefinger. 'No logic.'

'What?' With my luck, Davy was thinking, this fat old git'll turn out to be her father.

'Ask me about her,' Leonard said. 'Anything you like. I know everything about her.'

'How come?'

Davy eyed Leonard side-on. His gut, his pate, his white stubble.

'I've been going in this place for years. I know all the girls who ever worked in there.'

Davy felt little inclination to have any kind of conversation with Leonard, least of all a conversation of a personal nature. He said, 'I don't think there's much point in discussing it.'

'OK,' Leonard said, 'I'll tell you one thing, though.'

'What?'

'Women do not have logical minds. You hear me? No matter what they do, no matter how they try. That's just the way it is. I mean, how many great thinkers do you know of that are women? Any?'

Davy shrugged. 'I dunno.'

'None.' Leonard folded his arms across his chest. His expansive gut bulged out under the weight of them. He continued. 'This girl hates men. Why? Because nature has cursed her and given her a fanny. Because men can think in ways that she can only dream of. Ways that she can't.

So she hates men.' He stabbed at Davy's arm with his finger. 'So we must all suffer.' He paused and then added, 'I see it every day.'

'How's that?' Davy was interested, in spite of himself. But already Leonard's mind was elsewhere.

'Here is the picture I have.' He drew a square, mid-air, with his hand. 'Here is my information. She buys a paper every day. Does she read it? No. Only turns to the back and looks at the sports.'

He swivelled around and peered in through the window of the café, towards Jodi, who, true to form, was still leaning against the counter and staring at her paper. Davy stared too. He noticed that she was reading a big paper, not a tabloid.

'She has a large family. Four brothers. Hungarian. All older.'

'What's she reading?'

Leonard rolled back on his heels.

'Chess.'

'In the paper? I've never seen chess in the paper.' As he spoke, however, he had a vague recollection of having seen a black and white chess board on the back pages of proper papers.

Leonard said, 'See how she does her hair? See how her uniform is? All neat. Clean shoes?'

Like a bloody Fascist, Davy thought, feeling ashamed of the impulse in himself that had caused him to find her attractive.

'Everything is as it should be.'

Davy interrupted. 'She can't hear us out here, can she?'

Leonard shook his head. 'Wouldn't notice if I took out a gun and shot you. See her face.'

Davy turned and peered in through the window again.

Jodi stood by the counter, as before, reading, but her face, he noticed, was white, pointed, tensed, focused, bloodless.

'What's wrong with her?'

'Sex.'

'What?'

Davy laughed sharply, with embarrassment. Leonard pummelled the palm of one hand with the fist of his other, a gesture that needed little interpretation.

'Know what I mean? All those brothers. She wants to be like a man. All straight and neat and everything clear in her head. Silly bitch.' He licked his lips before adding, 'Ripe for the plucking.'

Davy noticed that Leonard's fringe, originally white, had been stained a sickly yellow from nicotine. Also a small funnel on his upper and lower lips, on the right hand side of his mouth where he characteristically held his cigarette. This man, he thought, is a bloody animal.

Jodi was still leaning against the counter. She was memorizing several of the moves in the Short/Timman match. Originally she had believed that chess was a game that invited skill, wit, spontaneity. But now she knew that the only way to contend at a serious level was to learn, to revise, to memorize, to plan and to structure. Prepare as if for war.

Jodi had three brothers. Her parents were Romanian. All had played chess from a very young age. Her father was an exceptional player. None of the other brothers had ever beaten him. Only she, Jodi, had managed this once, aged thirteen. It had been the best and the worst day of her life.

Her father had said, 'Do you know how you beat me, Jodi?'

'How?' She smiled up at him, exultant.

'Puberty. You have turned into a woman under my very nose but I didn't notice. When you moved your knight and left your Queen unprotected I thought: she's lost it, she's not concentrating. I let my guard down. I didn't see the move for what it was: sensuous, ridiculous, gregarious. Very, very feminine.'

Jodi had stared at him, unsure how to react. She thought, is this good or is this bad? She still asked herself this question: *Good or bad?*

Leonard nudged Davy in the ribs with his elbow. 'Once I listened about how she went to a pub to play chess with this famous English champion. Crazy man, long hair, glasses. I forget his name. Anyway, all the tables in the pub had boards. He played five games all at once, ten games, just walking between tables. She played four moves . . . one, two, three . . . and he beats her. Just like that. Easy!'

'So what happened?'

Leonard laughed and shook his head. 'She says, "I'll learn every move it's possible to make. I'll read every book. I'll see a whole game in my head before it's even played." Now she says she can play a game without even looking at the board.'

Davy felt suddenly ashamed. I asked her out, he thought, and I didn't know any of this. Imagine, all these things going on in her head and I couldn't even have guessed at them. He stepped away from Leonard and moved back towards the doorway of the café. He saw Jodi through the glass in the door. He felt a sudden, incredible, horrifying desire to consume her entirely, to take her and to make all those strange, abstract, alien parts of herself his own. He wanted to drink her down in one, like she was the liquid in a can of fizzy drink that could quench his thirst and bite into the back of his throat all in a single, thorough, rushing gulpful.

Jodi sensed a figure hovering around just outside the café, near the door, a blur beyond the edge of her paper. She had ten moves worked out in her head, one after the other. She *had* to keep them in. Order. Symmetry. Design.

Her own private moves were there, too, in the back of her mind.

I will never dance with a man.

I will never make love.

I will never marry.

I will never bear children.

She sighed as she put down her paper and glanced up towards the figure in the doorway. She sighed but she felt not the slightest twinge of regret.

And then she noticed that it was Davy standing in the doorway. Davy? Was that his name? And then she noticed that he had bright green eyes. It was her move.

Bendy-Linda

Belinda was well acquainted with the fact that the tortoise was a protected species, but this information could hardly be expected to improve her opinion of these silent, shelled, sly, *old* creatures.

She had joined the circus at eighteen, when she was awarded an E grade in her history A Level and an F in physics. Six years ago. Now she travelled the length and breadth of the continent, performing her gymnastic feats. She could start off doing a back-bend and end up with her head sticking out from between her own thighs. People at the circus called her Bendy-Linda, and the single question that she was asked more than any other was: *What is it like to perform cunnilingus on yourself*? To which she would usually reply, 'Depends how long it's been since I had a bath.'

Bendy-Linda also had chief responsibility for the performing parrot troupe: seven parrots which she dressed anthropomorphically and had taught to don and doff hats, hold up miniature papers, kiss each other – birdy, beaky kisses – and dance in time to specified tunes. They also talked. They said, 'Hello there', 'Milk and no sugar', 'May I have the pleasure?' and 'Great weather we're having.' She believed that these few sentences and phrases offered the key to a perfect life. A parrot utopia.

Belinda's main problem with the birds was to keep circus people, and others, from using inappropriate language in front of them. One bird had learned how to say 'Bloody Hell' and had been forcibly retired from the troupe as a consequence. Swearwords were like fireworks: much brighter and louder and sparklier than other language. Both children and parrots – those tiny sensualists – were irresistibly drawn to them, couldn't wait to wrap their tongues around them.

There were nine acrobats and tumblers at the circus, all told.

'The turnover of staff in this field has always been rapid.' This was Alberto, circus ring master and manager.

Belinda stared at him, unsmiling. 'I suppose that goes with the territory.'

Alberto nodded, not truly comprehending. *Turnover*, Belinda felt like saying, it's a joke.

Alberto was introducing her to a new tumbler. He was tall, thickset, blond; physically unlike your average acrobat. Alberto said, 'This is Marcus. He's French.'

'Hi.' Belinda offered him her hand. He took it and squeezed it gratefully, but said nothing, only smiled. Belinda smiled back and said, 'We usually all go out for a meal when a new acrobat joins. Pizza or something. It's a tradition. Are you keen?'

He nodded eagerly.

'OK, I'll arrange it.'

The following evening, a large group of them were filling out a significant portion of a local brasserie. Belinda sat to Marcus's left. On her left was Lenny, who in her opinion was a workaholic and a bore. He was analysing one of their routines. 'The first set of tumbles,' he said, his tone rigorous, 'come from nowhere. It's like the floor exercises in a gymnastic competition, lacking a certain fluidity, a certain finesse. I mean, there are no hard and fast rules in this business.'

Belinda looked at him, her blue eyes sombre and unblinking.

'Anyway, the tempo's all wrong.'

Choosing her moment carefully she said, 'Lenny, let's not talk about work all night, OK?' She turned and took a glass from a tray that was being proffered by a waiter. 'Pernod. Excellent.'

She focused on Marcus. 'How've your first couple of days been? I haven't seen you around much, apart from at practice and the show.' She had seen him at practice in his slinky French lycra garments. At least a foot taller than any of the other men, but gratifyingly agile.

Marcus took so long to respond to her enquiry that she almost came to the conclusion that he spoke no English at all. But eventually he said, 'It was . . . all fine.' He spoke slowly and laboriously. The effort of it brought tiny specks of perspiration to his upper lip. Belinda stared at him, wide-eyed. He's drunk, she thought, and it isn't even an hour since the matinée.

The waiter moved over to Marcus and offered him the tray. Marcus selected a bottle of beer, glad of this distraction, and drank down a hurried swig of it. Belinda said coolly, 'You're unusually tall for a tumbler.'

He nodded. 'Yes . . . I am.' After an inordinately long pause he added, 'Five foot . . . nine.'

He seemed to be relishing his words and observations with a drunk man's delight. Belinda had been tipsy herself on several occasions and was well acquainted with the feeling of intense gratification that the performance of everyday feats accorded one while in this condition. The brain works so slowly, she thought, that opening a door or saying hello are transformed into tasks of terrible complexity.

Marcus put his beer down next to his plate and started to say something else, but before he could complete his sentence, she had turned away, towards Lenny, and had begun to discuss the rudiments of their early tumbling routine with him in some detail.

Later that night, when Belinda attempted to enter her trailer, the door wouldn't slide back smoothly, but jammed when it was half open. She stopped herself from saying anything worse than 'Darn!' adding, 'Needle and thread,' for good measure. (The parrots were tucked up next door, covered for the night but ever vigilant.) She then groped around blindly in the doorway until her hand located a tortoise shell. You little swine! she thought, tucking the tortoise under her arm and reaching inside her pocket for a lighter to ignite one of the lamps.

Once the lamp was lit she kicked the door shut behind her. The tortoise was still under her arm, tucked snugly there, held dispassionately, like a newspaper or a clutch bag. His head and feet were completely drawn in.

This creature had once belonged to her grandmother and was called Smedley. Belinda dumped him down on to the floor again. He scuttled away instantly.

When Belinda had taken possession of Smedley, two years ago, she had been misguidedly under the impression that tortoises were no trouble. They hibernate, she was told. They're one of those creatures that don't need any attention. She couldn't reconcile this description with her own particular specimen. He certainly didn't seem to bother hibernating. In fact he appeared to have difficulty in sleeping at all. Most of his time was spent powering around inside her van, his head fully out, stretching on scaly elephant's skin, his feet working ten to the dozen. He took no interest in things, only walked into them or over them. Even his food.

Belinda's grandmother had owned Smedley for thirty-five years. He had lived in her garden during this time, as happy as Larry. Belinda had been given him, in accordance with the will, and a small financial sum concomitant in quantity with thirty-five more years of carrots and greens. Interest linked.

Twenty-four and thirty-five. She calculated these two numbers every time she caught a glimpse of the tortoise, scuttling from the kitchenette to her bedroom, emerging from under her sofabed. Fifty-nine. I'll be fifty-nine years old, she thought desperately, when that bloody creature finally kicks the bucket. It was as if the tortoise had already stolen those years from her. I'll be sixty, she thought, I'll be retired. I won't even have the parrots any more. I won't be able to do back-flips or walk on my hands. Smedley had taken these things from her, had aged her prematurely, had, inexplicably, made her small trailer smell of Steradent and mothballs.

It had been ten thirty when she'd returned. At ten forty someone knocked at her door. She pushed her slippers on, pulled her dressing gown tightly around her and yanked the door open. It was Marcus.

'What do you want?'

She stared into his face, slightly taller than him now, standing, as she was, on her top step. He said nothing, only handed her a note.

'What?' she asked again, taking it.

He bowed, low and formal, then walked off.

Belinda sat down on the top step and unfolded the note. It was written on onion paper. She always found onion paper quite peculiar. So light, so oniony. Very French.

The note said:

Good evening Belinda,
Eugenie told me that you thought I was drunk at dinner. Alas, no. I suffer from a speech impediment, a stammer, which in times of social tension can become terribly pronounced. I apologize if this minor problem irritated you in any way. I can assure you that it irritates me in many ways, but, as they say, such is life. N'est-ce pas?
Marcus

Although the tone of Marcus's note, the night of the dinner out, had been anything but hostile, Belinda spent the following five days trying and failing to apologize to him and to worm her way back into his affections. She found it extremely difficult to talk things over with a person who was virtually monosyllabic.

Because Marcus spoke so very little, he gave the appearance of listening much harder than your average person. Did he listen? Belinda couldn't decide. It felt like he did. She noticed how he became a kind of father confessor to all the tumblers, the acrobats, some of the clowns, the most beautiful tightrope walkers. He didn't strike her as particularly French. His accent – the rare smatterings that she heard – didn't sound especially Gallic.

In fact, both of Marcus's parents were English. They were a couple who had taken advantage of the Eighties property slump in France and had emigrated when he was eight. He was now eighteen. His stammer in French was much less pronounced than in English, which struck him as rather strange.

One thing his stammer had taught him, however, was never to waste words. In general he tried only to say things that were incisive and pertinent. He preferred to avoid chit-chat. When others spoke to him, he slashed out gratuitous noises and phrases in his mind, analysed what they said, not with the gentle, non-judgemental sense of a confessor, but with the practised, cool, steady calm of a surgeon. For instance:

Larry says: 'Marcus, tell me straight off if you think I'm out of line here, but I bet you'll find that the double back-flip after the handwalking stuff isn't strictly necessary. I mean, it's great and everything but just a little distracting.'
Marcus hears: 'Don't upstage me, new boy.'

Eugenie says: 'Wow! Those lycra things are fantastic. They look so comfy. They really do. I just love blue. I love that shade. It's my favourite colour. Are they durable? I suppose they must be French. The French are *so* stylish.'
Marcus hears: 'Let me get into your trousers.'

Belinda says: 'You really must come and meet my parrots. How about it? Tonight? After the show. If you're busy though, don't worry or anything. I mean, don't worry if you can't.'
Marcus hears: 'I'm sorry.'

In fact, Marcus was slightly off the mark with his inter-pretation of Belinda's babblings. The truth of the matter was that Belinda found him to be both aloof and disarming. She, too, wanted to charm the pants right off him.

Marcus had, however, noticed several worrying characteristics in Belinda's behaviour that did little to endear her to him. The first was that she jumped – too easily, too freely – to conclusions. This implied a certain amount of self-righteousness, a nasty, bullying bullishness. Secondly, she completed his sentences, which was something that he especially loathed. He guessed that people who were prone to doing this thought that they were helping him in some way, but it only made him feel useless, gratuitous, inadequate. He'd think: What is the point of *me*, if it's so easy to predict what I want, so easy to complete everything I begin?

The third and final thing that Belinda had done which had both shocked and disturbed Marcus, had occurred in the pub several nights after the meal out. Alberto had taken Marcus to one side, late that afternoon, shortly after the matinée, and had raised with him the possibility that he and Belinda might perform together during Belinda's contortionist routine. Since hitherto Belinda had been the only contortionist at the circus, this slot had always been solo. Alberto was keen to have Belinda partnered during this section, and although Marcus was no contortionist himself, Alberto felt that his leonine good looks and strong physique would make him the perfect foil to Belinda's dark skinniness.

That evening, in the pub, Marcus started to mention this new possibility to Belinda as she sipped daintily at her Pernod. He said, 'Can we . . . talk about . . . your . . . contortions . . . ?'

Oh yeah? Belinda thought, and what's he up to?

Alberto had said nothing to her about his plans. She was none the wiser.

She stared at Marcus coolly, vaguely disappointed in

him but unsurprised. He was trying to talk again, but she saved him the trouble.

'Cunnilingus,' she said, baldly. 'Unfortunately, my tongue is the only part of my body that isn't double-jointed, otherwise I'd dispense with you boys altogether.'

She took another sip of her drink and eyed him over the top of her glass. He blushed. He tried to say something, but it wouldn't come out. He stood up, drank down his drink in one large gulp and left the pub. Now what? She stared after him, profoundly flummoxed.

Eugenie was lounging against Marcus's trailer, waiting for him to return. She was a small, pretty acrobat with long, red ringlets. She was thirty, single, an old hand at the circus, sexually voracious. As Marcus made his way towards her he was thinking: Damn Belinda! Damn her! She's the strangest, coarsest, crudest woman I've ever met. She just seems to enjoy frightening me, on purpose.

'Hello,' Eugenie grinned at him. 'I've come around to borrow a cup of sugar.'

'Sure.'

She wasn't holding a cup. He unlocked his trailer and went inside, then emerged within seconds, holding a teacup full of sweet, white granules. He offered her the cup but she didn't take it.

'You're so literal,' she said, still smiling. 'I like that in a man.'

'Thank . . . you.' He inclined his head graciously. After a pause – not thinking to invite her in – he said, 'Be . . . linda.'

'What about her?'

'She's . . . rude.'

'She is?'

'I find . . . her so.'

Eugenie shrugged. 'You must just bring out the worst in her.'

Marcus considered this and then said, 'You think?'

'Maybe.'

'Why?'

She took the cup of sugar from him and said, 'You want to come and have some tea with me? Or coffee?'

'No . . . I . . .'

His stutter was so pronounced that Eugenie didn't wait around to listen to the reason for his refusal. She didn't mind. 'OK,' she said, phlegmatically, handing him back his cup. 'Some other time.'

Marcus sat down on his top step and stared into the cup. Thousands of grains. Mixed in with the pure, white granules were two extraneous tea leaves. That's me and Belinda, he thought. The world is full of millions of people, all friendly, all benign, the same. Then there's the two of us, destined not to get along. Belinda and Marcus. Both in the circus, this small circus. Both tumblers.

He felt relieved that his early and mid-teens had involved a longstanding but secretive intimacy with American *Playboy*. He was prepared for Belinda's lewdness, her crudeness. His father had kept an entire suitcase full of them in the attic which he had pilfered whenever he felt the inclination. Also, he had taken Latin at school, which in certain situations he found to be an invaluable linguistic tool. *Cunnus* – vulva. *Lingere* – to lick. Like choking on an oyster.

'Hi,'

Marcus looked up and almost dropped his cup. Belinda smiled at him. 'Look, I wanted to apologize. I guess I must've shocked you earlier.'

147

'No . . .'

'Well . . .' She focused on the strong, firm line of his jaw, its determined progression from behind his ear to the tip of his chin. 'I just saw Alberto.'

'Ah.'

'I don't suppose you want to come and see my parrots?'

'I'm . . .'

'Allergic?'

'No . . . I'm . . .'

'Busy?'

'No.'

'Go on, they're very friendly.'

Inside the parrots' trailer it was cool and dark. Belinda lit a lamp but kept the flame down low. 'It's bed-time for them really. I like them to be well rested. Otherwise they get cross and uncooperative.'

Marcus had seen the parrots already, in the big top. He thought them quaint but unnecessary. One day he hoped to work in a human circus, a wild circus where the performers did stunts on motorbikes and didn't use animals – camels with lopsided humps, sad, fleshy elephants, poodles with full wardrobes. Parrots.

'You like them?'

'I . . .'

'You don't like them?'

'No . . . I . . .'

'You like animals?'

He sighed. 'Yes.'

She said, 'My trailer's adjoining. We could have tea if you like.'

He shrugged.

Belinda opened a door and led him through. Her trailer

was identical to his, only full of stuff: posters, trinkets, an extra wardrobe.

'Sit on the bed,' she said. 'I don't ever bother making it into a sofa. Too much trouble. Watch the legs are out properly. It has a tendency to collapse.' She filled the kettle.

Marcus didn't sit down immediately. First he inspected some of the photographs on her pinboard. 'These are . . .'

'Me. Yes. When I was a kid. I got gymnastics medals. I was nearly in the Olympics but I sprained my wrist very badly two weeks before. I cried for a month.'

The pictures were eerie. Belinda at eight, ten, fourteen. Belinda doing headstands, handstands, flying on the high bar. Belinda with no breasts, mosquito bites, breasts like tiny buds under the thin fabric of her leotard.

Little girls; gymnastics. He always found this combination vaguely unsettling. On television, with their stiff backs, pointed toes, determined visages. Obscene. Tumbling was different. Better.

'Coffee or tea?'

'Coffee.'

He sat down. The bed collapsed.

'Merde!' This word slid out of his mouth as quickly, as smoothly as an angry cat escaping the arms of its owner.

Belinda stopped what she was doing, turned around and then started to laugh at him, at his clumsy disarray. She said, 'You aren't hurt, are you?'

He shook his head and dragged himself up, then tried to rearrange the coverlet and cushions. Belinda turned back, still smirking, to complete her coffee-making.

This bed reminded Marcus in its construction of the deckchairs his parents had used at home; space-efficient but impossible to set up and make secure. He pulled out the metal bar that acted as the front legs and pushed

149

up the springs and mattress. As he lifted he saw the tortoise.

Initially, it looked to him like an exotic seashell, or a lump of wood, centuries old, glossed up by the touch of many fingers, many hands. Then he saw it shudder, noticed a head, four feet. He reached out towards it, expecting a reaction. None came. One of its eyes was open, the other shut. That couldn't be right. He tapped its shell. Nothing.

I'm going to have to tell her now, he thought frantically, that I've killed her tortoise. How will I tell her? After several attempts, he said her name.

'Belinda . . .'

'Yeah?'

She had put two cups on to a tray. She picked up the tray and walked towards him. 'You haven't managed to get the bed up properly yet?'

He stared at her helplessly, as endearing and muddy-eyed as a golden retriever at tea-time. He pointed towards the tortoise. Her eyes followed the line he was indicating.

'Smedley!'

She quickly slid the tray on top of her dresser and crouched down. 'What's happened to him?'

'The . . . bed . . .'

'He looks all squashed.'

Marcus thought this an exaggeration, but took into account the fact that he hadn't seen the tortoise before its misadventure.

'Is he dead?'

'I . . .'

'He looks dead.' She reached out her hand as if to pick him up but then shuddered and withdrew. 'I can't stand the idea of something being not quite dead.' She added tremulously, 'If he wasn't dead and I touched him and he moved . . .' The thought of this made her feel queasy.

Marcus was staring at her. She saw his face – his expression a mixture of guilt and horror – and realized that these few seconds were crucial.

'He's dead!' she said, and burst into tears.

'I . . . I . . .'

For once he couldn't think of anything to say. Usually he could think of things only couldn't say them. Eventually he said, 'Sorry.'

'Tortoises,' she said, 'are protected. Did you know that? I never really knew what it meant, though. Protected. I never really knew. He was my grandmother's. He lived in her garden for thirty-five years. He was called Smedley. He didn't hibernate, only ran about in my trailer. He wasn't terribly demonstrative, but he seemed . . . happy.'

Marcus stood up. He was eighteen. He didn't feel sufficiently senior, sufficiently adult, experiencd enough, loquacious enough, to be able to cope with this situation. He felt like phoning his mother, packing and leaving, joining that other circus, that *human* circus, that un-animalled circus. He could see it already, how good it would be.

Belinda sat down on the bed. It promptly collapsed again. Marcus had only propped up the bottom leg, he hadn't got around to securing it properly. Belinda scrambled up. 'Christ! If he wasn't dead before, he is now. Christ!'

She was still crying, but was already sick of crying. Her tears weren't sufficiently effective. He wasn't hugging her yet, wasn't comforting her. Why am I crying? she thought. To seduce him? That was the sum of it. She wondered idly if you could go to hell for emotional blackmail.

Marcus took a deep breath. 'The tortoise could be hibernating.'

Belinda stopped crying in an instant and said, 'Five words all in a row! Well done! Five words, just like that!' She then burst out laughing. 'Hibernating? *Please!*'

He was mortified by her laughter. She's evil, he thought. Absolutely insincere. Absolutely unprincipled.

He's only eighteen, she thought kindly. Poor bastard.

Marcus turned to leave, so furious now, so angry that he felt like fire, like liquid. 'Your face . . .' he said, struggling, choking, '. . . Chinese Dragon!' Then walked out quickly.

Belinda stopped laughing after he'd gone, stood up, walked over to the mirror. Her face was still mirthful but tear-smattered. Chinese Dragon?

He was right. She looked like one of those brightly coloured, finely painted Chinese masks, the dragon faces, covered in tears, but grinning, grimacing. A frightening face, apparently, but only, she supposed, if you were Chinese.

Belinda went over to lift her mattress, pulled up the bed and kicked Smedley out from under it. He slid about on the floor like the puck in a game of ice hockey. Click, slither, thud.

Oh, well, she thought, this could've been sad, but I really don't care. I could've shocked myself by caring, but I don't care.

She started to laugh again. Laughing was good for you. A kind of internal aerobics. Then she heard a voice, and it was not her own. 'Merde!' it said, and cackled. 'Merde! Merde! Merde!'

Belinda stopped laughing, her eyes tightened, and her mouth – quite spontaneously – performed a sudden, gorgeous, perfectly inadvertent back-bend.

Gifts

Jennifer, 42, had a special gift which God had given her – out of the blue – to compensate for all the things that had happened to her in the past. All the awful things.

Jenny had the gift of knowing that something had occurred – either nice or nasty, but usually nasty – straight after it had happened. If she trod on a dog's foot and it yelped, if the milk boiled over on to the oven, if she dropped a glass and it smashed. Well, then she would *know*. This was the gift that God had given her and she thanked God for it.

Jenny lived in a small complex of sheltered housing close to the big Safeways in Stamford Hill. She lived independently, but if anything bad happened she had a cord she could pull in her hallway, next to the door, so that someone else – the warden, Peter – would come along and sort everything out.

The only problem with this set-up was that Jenny refused to pull the cord. She would not. She referred to it as 'that fucking cord' and she would not pull it. It was a matter of principle. Instead, her neighbour, Naomi, would pull *her* cord on Jenny's behalf to call Peter over if she felt Jenny was in some kind of difficulty and Peter was needed.

Naomi was seventy-six years old and had a bad hip

and could, occasionally, be clumsy and hurt herself. Sometimes she had to be taken to hospital when she scorched her hand or slipped over when climbing out of the bath.

At these times, when Naomi was absent, Jenny knew that if she got into trouble then she would simply have to sit down and think very hard about all the terrible things that had happened to her and how God had given her a gift so that she should *know* about them.

Naomi called this type of behaviour 'self-indulgence' but Jenny was content to feel that she knew better. To see things clearly, to register, to comprehend, well, that was surely a great blessing.

Jenny had a temper. Of course she did. And when she saw things clearly, they had to be seen properly, and everything had to happen in a certain way. She had her routines. A break from a routine was always a bad thing. Any kind of hindrance or interruption was considered by Jenny to be unacceptable. Any kind of intrusion, unpalatable.

Chad, 38, of no fixed abode, had a problem with rejection. But like Jenny, God had given Chad a gift too. His gift was that he would see things of no value, things that other people did not want, things that others misguidedly considered 'rubbish' and he would immediately love them.

God had chosen to give Chad his special gift because Chad had had everything – a home, a family, a good education – but he had rejected them. God understood difficult equations. God understood that Chad had been offered everything on a plate but that Chad had tipped the plate over. That made him special.

* * *

Peter, the warden, 23, was very familiar with Chad, his comings and goings, his shopping trolley, his stink, his pilfering, his cold sores.

Naomi knew Chad too. She liked to watch him picking through the rubbish, early on a Wednesday morning. The bins and the bags were put out the night before – a shiny black cluster, buzzing and rancid, ready for collection.

Jenny knew nothing of Chad. This was probably for the best.

Unfortunately, in October, when the leaves on the trees were starting to crisp and golden, Jenny's doctor decided to change her medication. He cut it down. He expected her to try to get through the night without her extra tablet.

So now, in the dark, she'd hear the clock ticking. So now, before dawn, she'd hear the birds singing. So now, after sunrise, she'd hear the cars on the main road close to her flat and the vans pulling into the unloading bay at the back of Safeways.

She even thought she could hear the drivers having a morning smoke, taking their fags out, the click of the lighter, the deep inhalation and the tinkle of the embers as they took their first drag. She convinced herself.

Wednesday morning, six forty-three precisely, Jenny heard something else. Much closer.

Outside, beyond the hawthorn hedge, Chad was carefully undoing the plastic knot on the top of a refuse bag. At first Jenny thought he might be a local stray, a cat, but when she listened more intently she decided that his technique was too deliberate, too careful for a creature with claws, too guided and thorough. So she threw off her blankets, clambered from her bed, walked to the window and gazed out. Beyond the hawthorn she saw Chad. Chad had gained access to the bag's contents. He'd found a broken saucepan which Jenny had snapped the handle off the day before. He was staring into it and he was thinking: is it big enough to use as a planter? For a small tomato plant? Shall I store it in my trolley? Shall I?

Jenny rapped on her window with the back of her knuckles.

'Oi!'

Chad looked up. Jenny stood at her window wearing a well-worn winceyette nightdress. The top two buttons were undone. Her navel was visible through a gap between the third and fourth. She had blue rings under her eyes. She hadn't slept properly for almost a week.

Chad stared at Jenny for several seconds, grimaced, returned to the bag, as though its contents held infinitely more interest for him than she did. Inside he found a wafer-thin slither of soap. In his trolley he had a self-assembled soap-cluster-ball which he'd created from just such soap remnants. It was almost as big as a cabbage.

Jenny opened her window and leaned out of it.

'Oi! Leave off!'

Chad looked up again, focused on Jenny, drew his lips back away from his gums and showed Jenny his teeth. They were brown and slightly peggy. It was an ugly expression, like the kind of face an ill-natured cur might pull. A snarl but nothing special.

Jenny gasped, slammed her hands on to her hips, marched into the hallway, appraised her emergency cord. Her fingers twitched but she didn't touch it. Instead she walked back into her bedroom, pulled on her dressing gown and returned to the window.

Chad had completed his dalliance with the bins and was now beating a slow retreat, disappearing from view, pushing his trolley with a combination of dignity and finesse, his back straight, his matted head held at an assured, an almost saintly angle.

Jenny slammed her window shut, piqued and disgruntled. Chad, she just *knew*, was a thief and a parasite.

'He's a magpie,' Naomi said, hours later, somewhat bemused by Jenny's fury. 'Don't get so worked up over it.'

'That's my stuff he's picking over,' Jenny retorted. 'My stuff.'

'Don't get so angry,' Naomi whispered, hoping to calm Jenny by speaking quieter. 'He doesn't mean any harm. He's only a tramp.'

'It's mine!'

'Shall I call Peter?' Naomi wondered out loud.

'My stuff. Private stuff. You know . . .' Jenny thought of something and stopped scowling for a moment.

'. . . You know, sometimes people go through your bins when they want to find things out about you. And then sometimes the people whose bin it is calls the police.'

Naomi smiled patiently at Jenny who was still wearing her dressing gown and pink mules.

'Michael Barrymore!' Jenny yelled triumphantly. 'They did it to him! Going through his bins to find out stuff! All his leftovers and everything covered in tea-grains and bits of potato peelings.'

'You mean newspaper people, Jenny,' Naomi said. 'That boy's only a tramp. He's been going through our bins for as long as I can remember. You couldn't call the police. They'd laugh at you. He's not breaking any law.'

'He's like dirty vermin,' Jenny said, 'a rat or something.'

Naomi went into her kitchenette for a glass of water. She returned and handed it over to Jenny. 'Taken your pills yet today, Jenny?'

Jenny took the glass but didn't drink the water, only stared off into the distance.

'Coming for how long?' she asked tremulously. 'How long?'

'As long as I can remember,' Naomi reiterated, then added, 'I'll tell you what he's got in that trolley of his. He's got a ball of soap almost as big as your head.'

'What?' Jenny's eyes refocused. 'Huh?'

Naomi made the shape of a ball in the air with her hands. 'He gets all the soap, see? All the last bits of soap from the bins and he presses them together to make a big, round ball.'

Jenny was confused, Naomi could tell, so Naomi went into her own bathroom and brought out her soap. 'See? When soap gets wet for a while the bottom goes soggy, then if you push it on to another piece they get stuck together when they dry, and that way he's made a big soap ball from all the last, little bits. I've seen him take it out of his trolley. Big as a football.'

Naomi looked up from the bar of soap she was demonstrating with. Jenny's expression was stiff and cold, frosted with disgust.

'Not *my* soap,' she said, shuddering involuntarily.

Naomi rapidly backtracked. 'No,' she said, 'of course not.'

Jenny's eyes widened as the full implications of the big soap ball had their impact in that special Soap-Ball part of her brain. She imagined how intimate a thing a bar of soap was and also, this dirty man, and then the rubbing of the soap into one ball. It triggered something in her. 'Never!'

She sprang up from her chair, spilling water on to Naomi's carpet.

'Never!'

Naomi went and pulled her cord.

She'd been thinking about it, at night, when she couldn't sleep. The Soap Ball. Her privacy. That saucepan he'd taken.

She kept remembering all the things that had happened with the saucepan. How she'd bought it from Argos. A set of three. How she'd liked to boil eggs in it and cook spaghetti hoops. She kept going over the pan's history in her head; it was bought, it was used, it was broken. All in that order. And now he had it. What had he done with it? Her pan.

Wednesday morning she was up at five. Sitting on a chair next to the window, overseeing her rubbish bags in the pile next to the hawthorn. During the week she'd packed them so carefully. She'd kept thinking about what was rubbish and what was not, what she could throw out and what she could not. Only food and packaging and broken glass. Old newspaper.

Anything potentially useful, anything personal, she kept back. A threadbare face-cloth, a used toothpaste tube, an old hairbrush, an empty moisturizing cream bottle. Anything personal. These things she stacked on her kitchen table in a sad, useless little pile.

Six-forty on the dot, Chad trundled with his trolley into the crescent, pulled up next to the pile of bags, paused, chewed his lower lip, inspecting them. Jenny pushed her face so close to the window that she steamed it up with her breath and had to pull back to wipe it clear. Chad kicked one of Jenny's bags gently with the toe of his boot.

Chad knew about bags. He was an expert. He knew

that the best kind of bag for his purposes was the kind of bag that jutted and stretched, that fought to contain something within that fought just as hard not to be contained. Jenny's bag felt soft and soggy, like it was full of bits of food and slush.

Naomi's bag, however, seemed distinctly more interesting. He untied it. Naomi's hands were frail and so Chad found her knots less difficult to negotiate.

Inside, on top, Chad found a mug tree. Natural pine, one of its branches missing, the base stained with something that looked like cod liver oil. He held it aloft. He smiled to himself.

Jenny had been intending to bang on her window as soon as Chad touched one of the bags, but when he didn't touch hers – only kicked it – she felt a loosening of her resolve.

Instead, she watched him inspecting the mug tree and enjoying a snout through Naomi's bag. Chad re-knotted Naomi's bag, after placing the mug tree in his trolley. Might use it at Christmas, he was thinking. Paint it green or something.

He left Jenny's bags alone. As if he knew! she thought, furious. Almost as if he knew! She stood up and tossed the chair she was sitting on against the opposite wall.

Chad heard the commotion emerging from Jenny's first-floor flat, glanced up for a moment, raised his eyebrows, sniffed, muttered 'Slag!' under his breath and then moved off.

Naomi, next door, eating her breakfast, chewing on a piece of bacon rind, heard the chair smash, jumped up and bolted towards her front door.

Peter looked at the growing pile of 'useful' rubbish on Jenny's table. 'So what's going on, Jenny?' he asked softly.

Jenny had made him a cup of tea but she was too angry to speak, almost. 'I can see that you're very uptight over something,' Peter added sympathetically, sipping his tea and wishing she hadn't added Hermesetas instead of sugar.

'Naomi's worried,' he said, pushing aside an eggbox and an empty cornflake packet so that he could rest his cup on the table.

'What's his name?' Jenny asked, her throat so taut she nearly growled.

Peter stared at her blankly.

'His name! Him!' Jenny yelled, picking up the eggbox, tearing it in half and then smashing it on to the kitchen lino.

'You know what I think, Jenny?' Peter said brightly. 'I think you and I should take a trip over to see Dr Eric this afternoon. Maybe cutting down on your pills wasn't such a good idea after all.'

'His name,' Jenny repeated, softly.

Peter took another sip of his tea. 'I don't know,' he said gently, after swallowing.

Later, Naomi told Jenny – in passing, not connecting anything with anything – that Chad's name was Chad. Jenny digested this information silently. *I knew it*! She told herself, victoriously, I just knew his name would be Chad.

Jenny was quiet for the rest of the day. In her mind she was thinking, Chad, Chad, Chad, Chad, Chad.

When she went to see Dr Eric, she purred and she simpered like a friendly kitten.

That whole week Jenny assembled all the best things she could find. Her favourite Catherine Cookson novels, her best lace tablemats, a sturdy teapot she'd not yet had occasion to use, a packet of felt-tips which she kept in a drawer for when her nephew called, a full bag of rice, a tin of Heinz baked beans. She lay out her array of goodies on her living room carpet. Then she placed them, one by one, into a black refuse bag.

Chad was late that Wednesday. He'd drunk a bottle of Tia Maria the night before which had left him feeling drugged and sweet and dumb. He was slower than normal as a consequence. And sticky.

It was almost seven when he turned into Jenny's crescent. From a distance he stared up at Jenny's window. He was fully aware of Jenny. He was sensitive like that. He had to be. He knew that for years he'd been looking in her bin and for years she hadn't cared but that now she did care. He knew that people were very prone to chucking things out and then feeling like the things that they'd abandoned still *belonged* to them in some sense. Stupid.

He saw Jenny's outline etched in charcoal against the windowpane. He didn't like being watched. Even so, he drew close to the bags, let go of his trolley, appraised the bags. One bag had been piled up on top. It had an interesting shape. He knocked the bag with his foot, kicked it aside and inspected some of the other bags below.

Jenny was dumbfounded. She was incredulous. All those good things in her bag, all her best things, and he had kicked it aside. If she squinted, she could see that he had opened another bag and was now cradling an old telephone directory in his arms. It was doused in something that looked like beetroot juice. Something cerise. Ugh!

Chad put the directory into his trolley, returned to the bag, pulled out an empty chocolate box, inspected it, put it back, tied up the bag.

He opened another bag, close to the bottom. From

within this bag he withdrew an old mop head and a plastic packet of carrots which hadn't been opened. He turned the packet of carrots over in his hand to double-check that they hadn't been touched, grimaced, noticed some mould on one of the carrots. He tossed the mop head into his trolley, tore open the plastic wrapping on the carrots and took one out. He bit off the mouldy end, spat it out, into the hawthorn, then proceeded to crunch his way through the remainder.

Jenny's eyes were wide, her mouth gaped. Those were *her* carrots. That was *her* mop head. This bag, her second bag, her rubbish bag, had been put at the bottom of the pile, specifically, so that Chad wouldn't get at it. How did he *know*? How?

Jenny raised her fist as if to knock on the window but stopped herself, froze, just in time, as Chad, at last, turned to the special bag, the kicked-aside bag.

As he untied it he was muttering to himself. He was saying, 'Something funny here. There's a reason. Something funny. That slag. Something up. Doesn't smell like rubbish. Bag's clean.'

He opened the bag. He pulled out a couple of lace tablemats. He folded them carefully and put them on the pavement to his right. He took out a Catherine Cookson novel and did the same. He took out the bag of rice, the felt-tips – these he held for a moment, he liked them, clearly – he took out the beans and the teapot. He liked the teapot, too.

Jenny sat at her window, watching him. She was very pleased indeed. This was right. This was good. She just *knew* this would happen. Absolutely.

What was her motivation? What was her plan of action? She didn't know yet. Hadn't decided. But it would be big when it came, and decisive, and when it happened she would *know* it had happened. Just so.

Jenny waited impatiently for Chad to put the stuff into his trolley. Everything was piled neatly on the pavement now, all correct and complete.

Chad appraised the pile of stuff. He then peered up at Jenny in her window through his lashes. He made a quick decision. He unzipped his fly, pulled out his penis, urinated strongly and freely on to the little pile of objects. He shook himself, put himself away, did up his zip. He walked over to his trolley. He departed.

Oh, Jenny was angry now. Oh, she was angry. 'I knew it!' she shouted out, through the window, through the wall, through the front door, at the emergency cord. 'I just *knew* he'd do that. I knew he would. I did! I did! 'Course I did!'

But a voice in her head said, 'Did you know? Huh? Did you?' So she ripped off a wide strip of wallpaper with her bare nails to prove to herself that she did know. She then discovered that she was having difficulty breathing. She felt dirty. Almost like he'd urinated on to her directly. Into her mouth. Her mouth! It was too much. She screamed and kicked her slippered foot against the wall again and again until she heard her toes snapping.

Problem was, Naomi – in her rush to get to her emergency cord – slipped on a plash of egg fat which had spat, seconds before, out of her frying pan and on to her kitchen lino.

At ten o'clock, when Peter called around to find out if she wanted any shopping, he discovered Naomi, crashed, incapacitated, bruises already flowering on her head and arms like bright kisses of cranberry. She'd fractured her fibia and sprained her wrist. She had slight concussion.

Jenny watched the ambulance departing from her

bedroom window. Naomi's hurt, she thought. I just knew that would happen. Chad did it. Chad, Chad, Chad, Chad, Chad.

She made splints for her toes out of toilet rolls, Sellotape and toothpicks. She'd nursed a bird once with a broken wing in just this way so she guessed that this process would be adequate. Her toes swelled. It hurt when she walked.

That night, while she slept – her foot propped up on a special pillow like a crown on a velvet cushion – Jenny dreamed of Chad's cold sores. She dreamed she was licking them with the tip of her tongue. They felt bumpy, like the head of a broccoli spear. They tasted like cough candy. She awoke, sweating, got up and drank four glasses of water in succession.

Thursday morning, Peter came to see her. Jenny did not make him tea. She was sitting on her sofa with a blanket over her legs. She said plaintively, 'I think I've got a chest infection. Bad catarrh.'

Peter came back later with some herbal lozenges, two lemons and a packet of Anadins. Jenny thanked him cordially.

It was a long week. Her toes hurt. The big toe especially. It remained swollen. The nail was cracked, but gradually Jenny found she could negotiate the hurdles and obstacles in her flat without too much duress.

She was waiting for Wednesday. She was waiting for Wednesday to come. Waiting, aching for Wednesday.

Chad almost didn't turn into the crescent. An instinct. Something warned him. Even so . . .

There were fewer bags out than usual. Chad let go of his trolley, stepped back a bit and peered up towards

Jenny's window. The window was bare. Jenny wasn't there. He was so surprised that he whistled to himself under his breath. *Toot-teet-toot!* He stepped forward and bent over to pick up a bag.

Jenny had always *known*, in the pit of her stomach, that some day her thick volume of Mrs Beeton's Cookery Classics would come in handy. The sound of Chad's jaunty little whistle was still resounding in her ears as she stood up from her position behind the hawthorn and smashed it down hard on to the back of his head.

He staggered left, he staggered right, tipped forwards, whoops! Clump. Jenny *knew* that Chad would fall over in just this way and she also knew that he would come to after a minute or so, open his eyes, blink rapidly and rub his forehead like he didn't know what the hell had hit him. Jenny planned to be back in her flat by then, Mrs Beeton stashed carefully among her other cookery books on her kitchen cabinet.

Unfortunately Chad didn't stir, didn't shudder or twitch for several minutes. After five minutes Jenny became slightly perturbed. She stared at him from her bedroom window. She pushed her window open and yelled down.

'Oi!'

Chad didn't move.

'Oi!'

Nothing.

Jenny's heart started racing. She didn't think this would happen. She didn't *know* this would happen. She didn't. She didn't. Nope.

Ha *ha!* Chad was awake but lying still as a corpse. He was so happy. He could hear Jenny's voice, low and then fluting, calm and then jumbled with fear and fright and mortification. He lay as still as he could without stopping breathing. He pretended he was a piece of driftwood lying on a beach. He was full of mystery.

Jenny went into her hallway and stared at her emergency cord. She could not. She could not. Her hand . . . ooohh!

Peter came. Jenny was outside by now, struggling to pick Chad up and he was as limp as a broken wrist. Without asking any questions, Peter took hold of Chad's feet and Jenny held him by the shoulders. Between them they carried him upstairs, to Jenny's flat, into her bedroom, on to her bed. Chad felt the mattress give under his weight, could smell lavender water and cheap talc on the pillow.

Peter knew his first aid. He gave Chad the once over. Chad was enjoying being limp and lifeless, still driftwood, still inscrutable. Through his lashes he glimpsed Jenny standing in the doorway, chewing her nails. He was laughing inside.

'Do you know what happened, Jenny?' Peter asked, eventually.

'Uh.' Jenny had been wondering whether cold sores were contagious, whether to get a tea-towel and prop it under Chad's head so that he didn't infect her pillow.

'I saw him,' she said slowly, then quickening up. 'I saw him bend over and then just fall, like. I *knew* something bad would happen. I could tell from the very first time I saw him.'

Peter sighed. 'Maybe I should call an ambulance –' He paused and then added, 'What happened to your foot, incidentally?'

'Uh.' Jenny looked down at her foot as though this was the first time she'd noticed anything amiss with it.

Chad sat bolt upright. 'You lying cow!' he spluttered. 'Is this any way to treat a man?'

Peter and Jenny both turned and stared at Chad, agog. Before either of them could say anything, Chad said, 'I had a wife and a home and a good education. I had them. I gave them up.'

'Get off my bed,' Jenny said, 'you dirty piece of shit.'

'If I'm a piece of shit,' Chad said, not moving, 'then what does that make you?'

'You try and stop me!' Jenny yelled, turning on her heel and sprinting from the room.

Chad stared at Peter, frowning. 'What? Where's she think she's going?'

They heard the front door slam and the sound of Jenny's feet clattering down the stairs. Chad's eyes widened for a second and then he sprang up from the bed and ran to the window. Outside he saw Jenny lumbering over to his trolley and plunging her hands in it.

'The bitch!'

Chad spun around and ran for the door. Peter walked to the window and peered out. Down below, Jenny was elbow deep in Chad's trolley, pulling out pieces of clothing, coffee jars, blankets, old books, dried flowers, three bottles of brightly coloured nail varnish. Eventually she found the thing she was searching for and held it up, held it aloft like the most precious trophy. The Soap Ball! Chad's Soap Ball! *The bits of soap, where they've been, private places, him all dirty, a bit wet and then rubbed, and then rubbed, and then . . .*

Chad charged into the street. Peter saw his lips moving. *Give me that*! Jenny held the Soap Ball to her chest, with both hands. *Nope. It's mine*! Chad lunged at her. Jenny stepped aside. Jenny said *Keep away from me with your dirty hair. All this soap and you've never even used it.* Chad said *Give it me! It's mine!* Jenny said *You had a wife and you had a education, so you say, and now you go in everyone's bins taking their private things and their soaps and everything.* Chad stopped then, stood stock still. He stared at Jenny with an odd expression on his face. Like she was worthless and he'd only just realized it.

Peter turned away from the window. Suddenly he felt quite sick, a curious feeling in his stomach. He sat down for a moment on Jenny's bed to try to collect himself. You see, he'd just had a premonition and it had struck him with such sharpness, such clarity. He'd just had a vision. It was the future. Ten years. Chad and Jenny, living together in this small flat. The walls a different colour. Everything dirtier. Jenny had a broken arm. Chad had a drink problem. They were happy together. Happy! She was defective and he loved her and she *knew* that he loved her. She did. She did.

Peter stood up, gingerly.

Jenny held the Soap Ball. It was all she'd imagined. Heavy and spiky, like a deep sea creature, like one of those puffer fish that sometimes you saw dried and suspended in dusty old museums near to the coast.

Parker Swells

The first thing she noticed was his handwriting. She was taking classes, you see, in handwriting analysis. His name was Parker Swells. She thought it was a silly name, not a name she could believe in. And his handwriting sloped to the left, wasn't confident, was ill-constructed. There were breaks where there should be joins, no flow, no coherence.

Under Previous Experience – when she checked his application form – he had written: *Builder*. In one glance she saw how he'd left school at sixteen with no exams, but now . . . one two three . . . now he had eight O levels and four A levels. Maths, economics, sociology, physics.

But he was a builder. And you'd think, she thought, that if he was a builder then he'd consider how he wrote things, keep straight on the line, not dip below, and make sure that the overall effect was clear and true. You'd think so.

She'd only met him briefly, when she'd sat in on the interview. They'd liked him. He came over well, seemed nervous but didn't fidget. He had a habit of blowing his fringe out of his eyes. What could that mean? She scratched her ear. Maybe he needed a haircut.

Her name was Bethan and she was a personnel officer. She was responsible for the second interview, the recall. And in this arena she brought to bear all the things she'd learned at college and at night school, and on the job, naturally, about the corporation and the kind of person who'd fit best. The corporate man. Or woman.

Tell me, she'd said, on her quiz form, *which you would prefer if given the choice: a well-crafted gun or a beautiful poem?*

Tell me, she said, just underneath, *in your own words, what was the best thing that happened to you last weekend?*

Parker Swells was not his real name. He'd done things he'd regretted in the past thirty-three years, and he had a child in Norfolk that he didn't want to answer for to the CSA. No way.

It was a desk job he was after at one of the four big banks. He'd passed three lots of accountancy exams. He'd walked the first interview and this was his second. Filling in a quiz form full of patronizing psychological pish.

After inspecting the form for the third time, Parker wondered whether to write what he really thought or whether to write the kinds of answers he knew they'd like to hear. But how in-depth were these things? Could they tell he was lying if he did lie? Could they ascertain by the way you dotted your *i*s and crossed your *t*s that you weren't being wholly sincere? What exactly were they capable of, nowadays? His pen wavered.

Bethan had withdrawn to her office, through a door to the left. The door was ajar though and Parker could see her ankle and the toe of her black patent leather shoe. She had dark hair and brown eyes and she was going somewhere. No wedding ring. A lambswool polo-neck which clung at her throat as tight and sure as the skin of a banana. She was slim. She was untroubled. She could afford to think about why people behaved as they did. To judge. Her life had been exemplary. She needed no excuses.

Tell me, the paper read, *which you would prefer if given the choice: a well-crafted gun or a beautiful poem?*

He'd been a builder. He liked tools and a gun was a practical thing. He had no moral objection to firearms. But his hand, his right hand, had been badly damaged in an accident, and so, realistically, unless he could learn to aim and shoot with his left hand – as he'd learned to write, and that had been a battle – then it would be of no real use to him.

He was shy about his right hand. It was fingerless, supporting only a thumb. He kept it in his pocket or behind his back. People rarely noticed.

Parker picked up his pen with his left hand. He reappraised the sheet of questions. What did they want him to write? In a company this big and this brutal, he supposed the gun, really. And the way the place had been built, out of steel and glass, all smooth edged and modern. A gun.

Even so, he was only one person in this whole corporation, one piece, one part. And he had a gammy hand. And he had no real use for a firearm. He wasn't afraid of anything. He had no scores to settle. He didn't like loud noises, nor did his neighbours. Maybe the poem.

But Parker couldn't remember ever reading a poem. He'd read limericks. He listened to songs and memorized the words.

> My old hen, she's a good old hen
> She lays eggs for the railway men.
> Sometimes one, sometimes two,
> Sometimes enough for the whole darn crew.

He liked that.

*   *   *

Bethan picked up Parker's quiz form. In the gap under the question about the gun and the poem he had written:

Depends on what the company wants. If they want a troubleshooter, I can do that. Give me the gun. If they want someone with flair and sensitivity, I can do that too. Pass me the poem. I can be both of these things. I can be all of these things. I want everything. I want nothing. I am adaptable.

She pushed her hair behind her ear. He was evasive, she decided, and yet assertive. He was confident. But at the same time, he didn't feel sure enough of himself to opt for one thing or the other. Maybe he didn't like making choices. Maybe he didn't enjoy making decisions. He was slippery.

Her eye travelled lower. She sighed at the way he'd mixed upper case and lower case letters. She started reading again.

What was the best thing that happened to you last weekend?
Here he had written:

Good things often come out of bad. Last weekend I got a message from a friend of mine. His name is Josh and we met at night school. During the day he works for a tool-hire company. Josh is friendly with another mate of mine, Sam, and sometimes we kick a ball around together in the park on a Saturday.

Three weeks ago we were playing and I accidentally fouled Sam. I kicked his shin with my spikes and grazed it. It bled a little. We parted on bad terms, but worse things have happened, so I didn't think anything of it and waited with Josh down at the park for him the week after.

But Sam didn't show. The week after that, either. It started to bug me. Maybe he was angry with me. Maybe he thinks I'm too bullish on the field. Maybe he really hates me. All stupid thoughts, but I was so cut up about it, this falling out, I even tried to ring once but he wasn't in. I didn't have the balls to try again.

Anyhow, Saturday morning, Josh phones me. He tells me Sam's dead. They found his body in his flat. He'd been dead for almost three weeks. He'd had a brain clot or something, a massive haemorrhage. And sure, I was cut up about it, but at the same time I was happy because I knew, in my gut, that Sam hadn't been angry with me about the penalty after all, not really. We hadn't fallen out in the end. He bore me no grudge.

Afterwards, though, when I went to his flat with Josh to help sort through some of his stuff, I couldn't help imagining how the phone must have rung that time I'd wanted to speak to him, and Sam, sitting close by, on the sofa, dead, the TV still on, the phone ringing.

Actually before I run out of space . . .

Parker had drawn an arrow and had continued this answer on to an extra piece of paper.

'Tea or coffee?' Bethan asked, strolling into the room.

Parker looked up. 'Tea, white, two sugars. Thanks.'

When Bethan returned with his tea, she placed the cup on the desk to his right. She had small hands, he noticed, and on her wrist was a little charm bracelet. The ornaments hanging on it were all connected with animals – fish, mainly, but a ladybird and a robin, too.

Parker thanked her for the tea, watched the curve of her hip pushing against the black fabric that contained it as she walked from the room, picked up his pen, smiled to himself and then started writing.

I must just get to the point. I was helping to sort through some of Sam's things. Me and Josh and Sam's mother. We were all cleaning and packing and clearing out his flat. This was Sunday. I was in the kitchen, mainly, and the first thing I came across was a bag of shopping which had been dumped, on the floor, next to the fridge, still not unpacked. Stuff Sam had bought at Spitalfields market the day after our last match together. The day he died. Some sourdough bread, mouldy now, some beetroots, raw, a lettuce – slimed up – and a box of free-range duck eggs. White eggs, like hens' only bigger.

I was about to throw the eggs into the bin with the other food but then Josh came through and said, don't chuck them, take them home if they're still fresh. And they were. So I did. Imagine that. A dead man's eggs.

I took them home and I was unpacking them from their box and into my refrigerator. For the most part they came easily, but then one of them had cracked and the juice that had escaped had dried like adhesive and stuck part of the shell to the box. I yanked it up but when it pulled free the egg was heavier than the others had been and felt odd in my hand.

I looked at it, closer. I held it on my open palm and it was shaking. That little egg. Jerking and warm on my palm.

I sat down and I watched it. For two, three hours. And slowly, very gradually, it hatched.

Bethan turned over the sheet, ready to find something on the other side but the other side was blank. She had become quite engrossed. What an odd man, she thought, and stared fixedly at the sheets before her while using her free hand to fiddle, unconsciously, with the little charm bracelet on her wrist.

She tried to work out what the answer Parker Swells had given her meant. What did it say about him? His friend had died. He was sensitive – worried about the possibility of having injured or offended him – but how did that relate to a work context? Could it relate?

She bit her lip. Parker's reaction to Sam's death had been curious, kind of dispassionate. But he went along to clean his flat, to help out, so he was handy. Good in an emergency? And then finally . . . the eggs. That was strange.

Bethan reread the additional material Parker had added on the second page about the duck hatching. This was the part of his story she found most interesting. Again, she messed with the bracelet on her wrist, looked down at it for a moment: fish, fish, robin, shark, fish.

Sometimes Bethan felt she had to be like a private detective in her line of business. To discover things, to unearth people's secrets, to pluck at threads and see what she could unravel. To read significant signs and signals into the apparently superficial.

Parker Swells had confused her. She felt all fogged up. She inspected his writing again, the slope, the mis-links, the way he didn't close his *a*s and his *o*s. She delved into her bag and took out her college notes. She checked back on a couple of references. There were signs here, definite signs. Below the line, sloping left, the *o*s . . . He was a liar.

Parker didn't get his third interview. The letter they sent him – the people from personnel – said very little, only that they'd had plenty of applicants and they hoped he'd find success elsewhere.

By a strange coincidence, a week to the day after Bethan had dispatched her rejection letter to Parker Swells, she met him on the platform at Canary Wharf, waiting for a train. It was five thirty. She was on her way home to Bow. As she walked past him he said hello.

'Hello,' she said, and looked at him askance.

'Sorry, you probably don't remember me.'

'I remember you.' She smiled. 'The duck.'

He chuckled at this but added nothing. 'I was here,' he said, by way of explanation, 'on another interview. With another bank.'

'Oh yes?'

'Yes.'

He was handsome, she thought, in his own way. He had gappy teeth and green eyes and skin which had seen the sun. Leathery. But he was a liar.

The train arrived. The doors opened. Parker was actually in front of Bethan, but he stepped back and held out his arm. 'After you.'

She thanked him and moved forward and then she saw it. His right hand, completely mangled. He caught her expression. 'An accident,' he said, 'at work.'

She nodded. They climbed on to the train. 'It's ugly,' he said, with apparent unselfconsciousness.

'Were you left-handed originally?' Bethan asked, shocked and momentarily stuck for something to say.

'No. Right-handed, always. I had to learn to use my left hand. To write, to eat and everything. After the accident I found I couldn't work so effectively in a manual capacity. That's why I decided to go to college. To qualify for something else.'

Bethan nodded. 'I get it.'

She felt guilty. She was normally so perceptive. That was what she was trained for and paid for, after all. That was her job. To notice things. But she hadn't noticed this. It was down to her, finally, that Parker hadn't got the third interview. Down to her, reading too much into things. But was that it? Maybe the problem had actually been a *lack* of information.

He should have told her about his hand. This was the kind of detail the company needed to be acquainted with. Doubtless, she told herself, stroking and smoothing her own ruffled feathers, too little information and not too much had been her stumbling block.

'Are you still working as a builder?' Bethan asked, eventually, praying for the affirmative.

'When I can.'

'What kind of things do you do?'

'Laying patios, retiling, making paths, that sort of work. And building ponds.'

Bethan blinked. 'I've got some ponds,' she said, 'a big one and a little one. Two ponds.'

'I know. You keep fish.'

Bethan was beguiled. 'How could you know that?'

He pointed to her wrist. 'Your bangle. Full of fish charms.'

She chuckled. 'I gave myself away.'

'Not at all. I'm simply interested,' he said, 'in details.'

'Me too. Actually . . .' She looked out of the window to check where they were. Three stops still to go. 'Actually,' she said, fiddling with her bracelet, 'I wish I'd known about your bad hand. That might've affected the conclusions we reached on your second interview.'

'What kind of fish do you keep?' he asked, like he hadn't really heard her.

'Carp. Koi carp. Beautiful ornamental carp.'

'And what was wrong with my second interview?'

'Um . . .' She paused. 'We felt that your answers on the quiz were slightly unconventional. Like, uh, like, well, like my pond at home . . .'

'Your pond?'

'Yes. My main pond at home has my three best fish in it, but it's hard to see them because it gets greened up a lot. Algae and plants and what-not. I bought a filter for it, to keep it cleaner, but I haven't installed it yet.'

'And my answers . . .'

'Like the pond. There was something good in there, deep down, something interesting, but it was difficult to see, to decipher, and your writing . . .'

'Scruffy.'

'Yes.'

'I know.'

'I'm sorry.'

'That's OK.'

She cleared her throat. 'And the duck?'

'The duck?' he reiterated, looking surprised. 'Oh, the duck. The duck. It's doing fine.'

*　*　*

Parker lay on Bethan's bed with his arms crossed behind his head. He stared up at her light fitment. A heavy, glass lamp, yellow, the wiring, he noticed, coming slightly away from the cornice and the ceiling. He made a fist out of his damaged hand. He'd lost count of the number of women who had taken him into their beds simply because of this one, small, gorgeous imperfection. Sympathy was a powerful emotion. Might not seem it, but it was. And guilt.

Bethan strolled back into her bedroom. She was carrying a packet of biscuits and a couple of apples. She was naked. She bit into one of the apples and handed Parker the other. She sat down on the bed.

'We missed dinner,' she said, and grinned.

'How big is your garden?' Parker asked.

'It's tiny, really.'

'Do the ponds take up most of it?'

'Come and look,' Bethan said, and pulled on a T-shirt.

'I didn't build them, they were here when I bought the flat, so I thought I might as well put in some fish. Initially I just had goldfish and then one day I saw some carp at a garden centre and I thought they were so beautiful. So big. They come in every colour. See him? The gold one? Gold and white. He's called Samson. He's the oldest. The biggest too: I feed them by hand.'

Parker stared into the water. The ponds were antique and grand and well-established.

'That's a beautiful pond,' he said. 'Is it deep?'

'Very deep. Too deep. Sometimes the fish swim under and I don't get to see them for days. And see how murky it gets towards the bottom? That's why I bought the filter.'

'It's good, though,' Parker interjected, 'not to see the bottom. The fish must like to dive and disappear.'

'Only I haven't been able to set it up myself,' Bethan said, like she hadn't heard him, 'the filter. Too complicated. I'll show you it, if you like. It's in the shed. You might be able to give me some tips.'

She stood up.

It was late and Parker was pulling on his coat. She had given him the key to the side gate.

'I'd give you the house keys,' she said, 'only I've not got an extra set.'

He smiled at her. He found it strange that she'd have sex with him, let him inside her, but the keys to her home she couldn't quite trust him with.

'I wish you could bring the duck along while you're fixing up the filter,' she said, out of the blue, as he was walking through her front door.

'What?'

'The duck. He'd do well on my two ponds but I don't think the fish would like it.'

Parker laughed. 'There is no duck,' he said.

'What do you mean?'

'No duck. I made it up.'

She stared at him, her mouth open, barely comprehending. Eventually she said, 'But the duck . . . that was the best part of it.'

'Of what?'

'The story. The duck . . .' She looked flabbergasted.

Parker put his head to one side, still smiling. 'While I was filling out that quiz you brought me in a cup of tea, remember?'

She nodded.

'And I saw the bangle you were wearing, full of fish and birds and stuff. I thought the duck story would appeal to you. That was all.'

'So you lied on your application form?'

'Doesn't everybody? Didn't you?' Somehow, though, he thought he already knew the answer to this question. 'It doesn't matter,' he said. 'It's only a question of telling the right kind of lies.'

'Doesn't matter? Of course it matters.'

'You really want the full picture?'

His smile was strange, suddenly, and full of pain. 'You don't want the full picture,' he said, answering his own question. 'You wouldn't recognize the full picture if someone sat down and painted every tiny stroke of it straight on to your pretty hands and your silly face.'

'What's that supposed to mean?'

'You didn't know I was disabled but you came to certain conclusions about me because of my writing, you read into what I'd written things I hadn't said. It was kind of . . .' he paused and considered for a moment, 'kind of despicable.'

'Was it all lies?'

'Only the duck.'

'So you are a liar. I was right. I was right about you.'

He ignored this. 'Was I a liar,' he asked, 'before I filled in your stupid quiz form?'

She stared at him in silence for a while and then she put out her hand. 'Can I have my key back?'

'Why?'

'I don't want you fitting my filter any more. I feel weird about this now.'

'Don't be foolish. I'll fix the filter.'

'Give me the key.'

He laughed and handed her the key. She closed the door on his smiling face. She wrapped her arms around her breasts and shuddered.

It took almost an hour for the police to arrive. The constable who finally turned up was thickset and blond-haired and held his hat under his arm like it was a baby. He had a habit, Bethan noticed, of wiping his palms on the side of his thighs. She invited him in.

He took out his notebook and waited for her to say something.

'I came home from work,' she said, 'to discover that someone had broken into my property, through the back gate . . .'

'Did they force the lock?'

'No. I think they broke the lock and then replaced it. I found some new keys posted through my letterbox.'

'Someone changed the locks and then posted the new keys through your letterbox?'

'Yes.'

'Do you happen to know who might have done such a thing?'

'Yes. I know who did it. He's called Parker Swells.'

Bethan spelled Parker's name out loud and checked as the constable wrote it on his pad.

'I have his address and all the details you could want about him, only everything's still at work . . .'

The policeman nodded. 'And what, exactly,' he said, 'apart from changing the lock on your back gate, did he actually do?'

'Come outside.'

Bethan took the police officer into her back garden.

She pointed. He looked around him. There was little to see. A neat lawn, flowerbeds, nothing amiss.

'He stole my ponds,' she said, her voice cracking.

'Your what?'

She pointed. He saw five, large, beautiful fish in a curious selection of small, clear-glass containers.

'He stole my ponds.'

Ponds, the policeman wrote down in his book. Stolen.

Bethan watched as he wrote this. His writing, she saw, was round and girlish and immature. She wished they'd sent someone else. He clearly wasn't going to prove competent.

'And why do you think he did this? Why did he steal your ponds?'

Bethan didn't know. She couldn't answer. She felt so ridiculous.

'He had a duck, a pet duck,' she said, eventually. 'Maybe he stole them for his duck.'

She glanced up and saw the policeman was smiling at her. She looked away.

'Those are beautiful,' he said, indicating towards the fish. She nodded. Her fish hung, suspended, in their small, plain glass bowls; tight and bright and golden. Their gills moved; in and out, in and out. Bethan could clearly see every tiny little detail now.